Fr Makeup to Murder

Jacky ROm

ISBN :
978-0-9562172-3-3

Illustrated by
Vicki Butcher

Edited by
Nikki Mead
First Published 2015
JAX PUBLISHING UK
www.jackyrom.com
FROM MAKEUP
TO MURDER

Jacky Rom

Acknowledgments

Wow! What an adventure! After writing five children's books my goal was to write my first adult classic crime suspense story. A very special thank you goes to Nikki Mead, who was constantly enthusiastic as she received samples of the Novel. Thank you for editing, questioning and loving Sandy and this story.

I would like to thank Mick Lennon, Ex London Met Murder Squad Detective and Leanne Verwijs, St Maarten Detective, for helping me understand 'Murder' and how to solve it. Your input was invaluable!

To Scott Gardenhour. Thank you for answering my technical questions about the true workings of a film set and for brightening my year with the suggestion of film rights, my life's dream!

To the Island of St Maarten, my second home and all the lovely people that love the Island like I do. Thank you for your input and enthusiasm.

Sandra Bernstein, although a fictional character, has now become real to me and I hope she has many more adventures around the world! I hope you enjoy it as much as I did writing it.

Contents

Chapter 1

'Hold those doors!' A loud voice boomed, 'I'm here!'

The air hostess on the American Airlines flight AA47 was about to close the heavy plane doors just as Sandy screamed rather loudly and came running towards her. It was the bellowing high-pitched voice, along with the colourful eccentricity of the woman that stopped her.

Sandy arrived at the doors like the cartoon Road Runner and skidded to a halt, her multi coloured hand luggage trailing behind her. Her hands barely managed to hold onto her trailing case, her handbag and a small holiday leather money pouch. The Air Hostess smiled at Sandy as she let her through the doors.

'Made it!' Sandy exclaimed whilst trying to catch her breath.

'Only just,' replied the over forty-five year old, over made up, stuck up air hostess with a permanent smile.

Sandy wasn't sure if this was just years of playing the hospitable hostess or if she had had semi permanent makeup that made her look ready to play the part. Sandy suddenly realised she was staring and shook her head a little.

Sandy tried awkwardly to remove her boarding pass from her over stuffed leather pouch, whilst still holding onto everything. At first she used her teeth to pull the offending piece of paperwork from its pocket on the side, whilst the air hostess moved from one leg to the other keeping her smile and pretending to be patient. *Of course she couldn't possibly think of helping,* Sandy thought. As the teeth didn't do the job Sandy decide to off load everything onto the floor to be able to show her boarding pass and get seated. Her designer handbag fell with a loud bang and her luggage landed in the same manner. The air hostess had the guile to say, 'Can I help you with that?'

Sandy just looked up from the floor where she had bent down to retrieve the fallen leather pouch with the elusive boarding pass.

'No thank you, I've got it,' and passed it over to the extended hand.

'Oh! You're in first class,' she uttered with her nose stuck in the air. Sandy wanted to say 'AND!' then flick her dainty ankles so she would fall to the floor, but decided just to smile and get to her seat as quickly as possible. She was aware twenty-five of the people nearest to her where watching for her next move.

'Follow me!' the hostess said.

Sandy retrieved her belongings and followed *Agatha,* as she had nick named her, up the aisle by turning left and walking through the business class cabin. Sandy was totally oblivious to the people she passed and clipped with all her different bags. *Agatha* stopped and showed Sandy her seat. Sandy dropped her oversized bag onto her seat and put her multicolored case in the overhead compartment. She totally ignored the looks of disdain from the other passengers and continued getting herself organised. With one huge sigh Sandy flopped into her seat as the seat belt sign lit up. The Captain's voice could be heard over the tannoy and it was time to go!

Sandy sat there reflecting on the last few tumultuous days. It had been a roller coaster ride through highs and lows and now it was time for her to start a new life. She was now fifty-two years old and had spent all her life as a Makeup Artiste. For the last fifteen years she had been working on a daily soap opera called 'The Helter Skelter' and even that gig had just landed in her lap one day. Sandy was a dreamer, a scatterbrained dreamer, who at the tender age of fifteen decided she wanted to be a Director, but with no idea how to make it. Her family where a traditionally middle class Jewish family whose only hope for Sandra was to make a good Jewish home for herself with a good Jewish husband, preferably a Doctor. The idea that their daughter wanted to be involved in the world of entertainment was as far away from their world as they could imagine. Sandra's dad was a Stock Taker. He went into business' each year, or when they wanted to sell, to value the stock. Now a dying trade as everything has become computerised. Luckily, Sandy's one brother was happy to take over the family business, leaving Sandra to follow her dreams, but without any guidance Sandra, as her parents called her, was left to her own devices. Sandy's mum was a homemaker. She loved to cook and tend the garden. Sandy soon realised that she wasn't anything like her mum and fought tooth and nail to be quite the opposite. She could still hear the dull tones of her mother saying, 'You need to get yourself a real job!, not run after silly dreams.'

This spurred Sandy to be resolute about her direction. All by herself she secured a place at the London College of Fashion, London's leading college for Makeup Artistes. Her reasoning was she would get herself trained, get on a film or television set and from there somehow became a Director. The tender thought of a fifteen year old! How wrong can they be? Sandy loved her time at the college and left with a new talent and air of London polish. Her first job was in Selfridges, the large department store in the middle of Oxford Street, one of London's busiest streets. Whilst working there she got a call from a friend about a job that was going at a wedding hire shop. They were looking for a permanent Makeup Artist to make up the brides. Sandy loved the idea and quickly made an appointment to be interviewed. She got the job and spent the next ten years working there.

One day, one of the more difficult brides she had looked after contacted her. She was a regular actor on the daily soap opera 'The Helter Skelter' and she needed a new Makeup Artiste as hers had just left to have a baby. It was that simple and once again Sandy fell into her next job. Helga Beaumont was a typical soap opera star. She loved the limelight and was a consummate diva. This was her third marriage. Her first husband ended up in prison for life for fraud, the second one left her for a younger model and this one was a fellow actor from a rival television soap, but Sandra didn't mind working for her, as she was her ticket to her dream of working in the television industry.

Through the years the show had become one the UK's biggest shows, regularly getting over five million viewers an episode. Now it was shown all over the world and had picked up multiple awards. Sandra was happy now being back stage and creative, she was happy with her lot. She had a lovely apartment in North London, which was only fifteen minutes walk from the studios. She had two cats Alphaba and Glinda and lovely neighbors who looked after the cats and her flat when she needed a break. Her parents still lived in the same house in Stanmore and her brother had now moved abroad to New Zealand with his wife and brood of three boys. Sandy tried to visit her parents at least once a month, but her schedule was grueling and she often worked a fourteen-hour day. Now, after over thirty-five years, her parents were proud of her achievements, especially the awards she had collected over the years for best makeup in 'The Helter Skelter', which were now displayed in their living room. However, just over a week ago she was working on the show when a runner came into the makeup studio and handed her a note. Inside it simply said: *Hi Sandy, can you pop and see me. John Tourmont.*

John was the show's Producer and this was the fist time in all her fifteen years she had ever been summoned to his office. Sandy put down the brushes she was cleaning and made her way along the main admin offices to John's door. She knocked, heard a scuffle and then John's secretary left the room rather disheveled. John was very well known for his amorous encounters and everyone just seemed to turn a blind eye. Sandy heard a deep 'Enter.' and she made her way in. John raised an eyebrow as he saw Sandy enter. Sandy had transformed over the fifteen years into a larger than life character. Her hair was bright red, not auburn but fire red and was normally adorned with some kind of exotic finishing. A flower, turban or large piece of material that seem to have a life of its own. Her clothes where hardly practical and seemed to be thrown together rather than masterfully chosen. Today Sandy wore a small black fascinator tilted on the left side of her head. A Chinese kimono that was tied by what looked like a curtain tie and black wide-legged trousers that covered her high-heeled boots. Sandy was always perfectly made up and would certainly never go out of the house without her full face on. She smiled as she walked to cover up how nervous she really felt and swanned into John's office. John regained is composure.

'Hi Sandy,' he said rather quietly. That unsettled Sandy, as she had never heard him be reticent about anything. In the fifteen years she had known him, he had always just said hello and then signed his famous Christmas card once a year. They had very little contact. Sandy sat down and waited.

John fiddled around with some paperwork and then looked up.

'I'm sorry,' he announced.

'Sorry about what?' Sandy questioned.

'I wanted to be the first one to tell you, as you've been her so long.'

Sandy started to worry. John was taking in riddles and was looking very sheepish.

'Yes?' Sandy urged.

'I am truly sorry Sandy, but we have got to let you go. The show has been pulled by the station.'

'Pulled?' Sandy repeated.

'Yes. Viewing numbers have dropped dramatically since we change time slots and we are closing on Friday. I wanted to tell you personally as you are one of our longest serving employees.'

'FRIDAY!' Sandy repeated rather hysterically. 'This Friday?'

'I'm sorry, Sandy. It's a shock to us all.'

Sandy stood up and said, 'Thank you for letting me know.'

As she went to walk out John said, 'I'm sorry Sandy, we all are. We have all spent most of our lives here, it's going to be hard on everyone.'

Sandy nodded and left the office.

Holding back the tears, she walked back to the makeup studio in a trance, thinking to herself, *what am I going to do?*

By the time she got to the door, she was none the wiser. Sandy could hear rumblings of whispers and as she opened the door it stopped. Inside there were three other makeup artistes milling around each of them, about twenty to thirty and agency workers not permanent staff like her.

As she walked in she realised the news was public knowledge, everyone else seemed to know before her.

Chris who was looking at her with a sad face said, 'I'm sorry Sandy, we've only just heard from the Agency. What will you do?' Sandy thought for a minute and on autopilot said 'I think it's time to see the world!' and made a dramatic exit.

She left the makeup department, closed the door, rested on it and took a deep breath. A calmness took over and it gave Sandy a few moments to think. She silently counted to ten and then once again opened the door and walked back to the makeup room.

'Ok, guys!' Sandy said loudly, 'We've got a job to do! We still have five days to go, so let's be professional and go out with a bang. If I know anything at all it's about how the show will go with a bang. If we are lucky our skills will be put to the test, so let's make sure we have enough blood in stock. I'll go and ask if the final scripts are available and when we can see them.' With that Sandy left the room, went into the ladies toilets and sobbed quietly.

Fate is a strange thing. They say one door closes and another one opens. In Sandy's case, this little hiccup in her career opened up a new and exciting world of possibilities. By the time Sandy had walked home on that fateful day her mobile phone started ringing. She thought twice about answering it as the last thing she wanted was to talk to sympathetic people. She looked at the phone and didn't recognise the number so answered.

'Hello, this is Sandy, can I help you?'

'Hi Sandy!' came the reply. 'Its Helga, Helga Beaumont. I hear you've just heard the news.'

Sandy wondered how Helga, one of the leading ladies from 'The Helter Skelter' had got her phone number and even more importantly why the hell she was calling her.

'Ah yes,' she answered.

'Well, I've got some amazing news and I'm hoping you'll be a part of it.'

'Ok, what is it?' asked Sandy quietly.

'I've been offered a part in a film,' Helga replied.

'That is great, but how can I help?' Sandy questioned.

'I've been told that I can choose my own crew and I would really like you to work with me. You have looked after me for years now Sandy and I wouldn't want anyone else doing my makeup, but there is one obstacle to get over,' Helga proclaimed.

'What's that?' Sandy asked.

You will need to be with me for the next twelve weeks... in the Caribbean!'

Sandy was silent.

'Hello, are you still there?' Helga asked.

'I'm still here,' Sandy replied. 'I'm just trying to take everything in. I've only just heard ten minutes ago that I have lost my job of fifteen years and now your offering me a new one, but if I want it I have got to pack up and fly half way across the world. I'm sorry it's all a bit overwhelming!'

'I know. I feel like that too, but as they say one door closes as another opens. So just think about it, but as it's Monday today you haven't got much time. You will need to fly on Saturday and we start shooting next Monday. Just call or text me tomorrow to let me know either way.' Helga hung up.

Sandy put the key in her door and opened it, she could hear her two cats playing and chasing each other. All of a sudden the enormity of everything that had happened caught hold and she dropped her bags, closed the door and leant up against the back of it.

'Hey girls!' She shouted to the cats, 'I think my life is about to change!'

Chapter 2

Sandy looked up as the seat belt sign went off. They were now flying at a high altitude and Sandy took a deep sigh and thought to herself, I've done it, I've really done it. I'm off on a new adventure! Sandy thought about the mad few days between the meeting, where she found out she didn't have a job anymore and now sitting here on the plane. It hadn't really taken long to make a decision, as she didn't really have a choice. How could she turn down the chance of working in the Caribbean for twelve weeks? It was either that or going to collect unemployment benefit.

Making arrangements to get going in four days was quite a feat, but thank goodness for Dave and Chris, her next-door neighbours. Not only where they happy to look after Alphaba and Glinda, they also agreed to look after Sandy's apartment. Once that was organised the rest was simple. See the parents, break the news, pack and off!

It was a nine-hour flight to get to Miami and then a two-hour layover, before her two-hour flight to a small Island called St Maarten, so she had plenty of time to think. For the first time in as many days, she sat and actually spent time thinking about her future.

Sandy's thoughts where all over the place as she settled in for the long flight. She thought about her past and queried her future, but she knew she had nothing to loose. At least twelve weeks in the sun can't be bad and to be paid a good wage at the same time was a bonus. She tried hard not to think about what would happen after she returned and hoped that working for this production company would give her a great start. So, she settled down to read a crime thriller. Sandy loved everything about crime television, film and novels. CSI, Law and Order, Bones, Castle and every other US Crime television show. A good thriller saw the time past fast. In fact she could see herself as a private investigator. She had a very logical mind and quite often realised who the murderer was well before it was announced. If she hadn't become a Makeup Artiste maybe she could have become a detective. Her hobby was amateur sleuthing. A lost cat, or stolen dog or even a local burglary was solved by Sandy. In her neighborhood she was well known as 'Solve It Sandy'. A title she hated, but she knew people called her that behind her back. She was often seen late at night on her computer investigating something or other.

Sandy started to read her book and dozed off. In what felt like five minutes, but was more like forty-five minutes, a hostess gently touched Sandy's shoulder and asked her if she would like a cup of coffee. Through her grogginess Sandy nodded. The hostess started to prepare the coffee when suddenly Sandy heard a strange voice say, 'Hurry up! Get a move on!"

It wasn't her voice and she was sure it wasn't the nice older lady she was seated next to. The hostess gave Sandy an evil look and said, 'I'm sorry madam, I am trying my best.'

'That wasn't me!' Sandy replied, apologising. Then she heard the voice again.

'Hurry up! Get a move on!' the voice repeated.

This time the hostess could clearly see it wasn't Sandy and gave her a curious look. Then the voice said, 'Time for bed! Time for bed!'

Sandy started to giggle and covered her mouth trying hard not to laugh out loud!

'I'm so sorry,' said the lady next to her, 'That was Monty, my parrot!'

The hostess didn't react and just gave Sandy her coffee and moved down the aisle.

'You've got a parrot under your chair?' Sandy asked the lady.

'Yes,' she replied, 'She travels everywhere with me, I've had her over twenty years. We were lucky she didn't say anything worse. She tends to repeat things she hears. She is very intelligent. I've covered the cage, which normally means she goes to sleep, but this is a long journey and I think she feels left out. She just wants to join in!'

Sandy and the lady chatted away and the time passed quickly. The lady introduced herself as Glynis and was off to Miami for the winter to stay with her son. Sandy was envious as Glynis informed her she spent at least three months a year in Miami with one child and three months in

New Zealand with another, taking Monty with her everywhere.

The safely belt sign came on again and this time its was time to land. Sandy buckled up and got ready for the landing. Miami airport was vast and Sandy had to ask for help once or twice before she found the gate for her connecting flight to St Maarten. She didn't have too long to wait before the plane started to board. This flight was only two hours long. She quickly got seated, as she was now an expert with her hand luggage and bag and leather pouch. She took the magazine out from the pouch in front of her and the very first story was all about the Island of St Maarten.

St Maarten is the only Island in the Caribbean that belongs to two countries. It is approximately thirty-four square miles and is shared between France and the Netherlands. It was divided into two in 1648.

The airport Sandy arrived at was modern and lovely and clean. The passport control lady was polite and said, 'Welcome to the friendly island!' as she stamped Sandy's passport. Sandy went straight through to pick up her luggage. Within ten minutes the luggage started to whirl its way around the carousel. It wasn't hard to spot hers as it all matched the loud brash carry on case. Three cases later, she had all her stuff together on a trolley and made her way through to the customs. No one was there and she went straight out into the arrivals area. As the double doors opened she was greeted by a plethora of people and tucked in the middle of about eight locals, all with car hire or holiday company logos on their t-shirts, was a short, white, spiky haired skinny, diva! He was holding a large card with the name Sandy Bernstein written on it and waving profusely. Sandy smiled and pushed her heavy trolley towards him.

'Hi Sandy!' he spouted as if she was a long lost friend. Sandy smiled and shook his hand as he carried on, 'Welcome to St Maarten, my name is Andy and I'm Miss Helga's PA.' He then took a little bow and carried on.

'Now let me help you with your stuff and we'll get going. How was your flight, has it been a long one?' he said all in one breath. He took Sandy's trolley from her and started walking towards the exit, still chatting. He took another breath, but not quite long enough for Sandy to utter a single word, and carried on.

'You will love it here, the weather is amazing and this production company cannot do enough to look after us all. I've only been here three days, but already it feels like home!'

Sandy just nodded and smiled as he carried on again.

'Now lets see, where did I leave the car? Oh yes, it's over there. By the way, you going to be hot in those clothes, I hope your bought some summer stuff, the weather here is amazing.'

Sandy just nodded again and followed Andy to the waiting car. He carried on talking, but as he had his back to her, she had no idea what he was saying until they got to the car and he turned round.

'Ok here we are! Now, Helga told me to take you to your Condo, let you get unpacked and rested then well all meet up for dinner.'

Andy looked at Sandy for a response, so Sandy uttered 'Perfect, lets get going!'

As Andy opened the seven-seater car door, she realised there was already someone in there.

'Whoops! Sorry, I forgot to say that we are just dropping some friends of mine off first.'

'No problem.' Said Sandy and started to get in as Andy put her luggage in the back.

There was a driver, two local people and a goat. Yes a goat. A bleating goat, which looked like he wasn't happy at being disturbed. Andy got in and closed the door as the car began to drive off.

It was hot and although the driver had the air-conditioning on, it was just moving the smell of the goat around. Sandy wanted to throw up, but tried to breathe deeply to keep the bile down. They started to drive up a large hill on what looked like a dirt track and Sandy refused to look out as goats and hills didn't bode well. Slowly, the car struggled to get up the hill and turned suddenly into a small side road.

'Here we are then!' Andy exclaimed as the driver stopped the car and opened one of the doors. The goat left first followed by the two friends of Andy. She wasn't sure how he had made new friends after only being on the Island a few days, but she didn't feel like asking.

'Now!' Said Andy. 'Let's get you home.'

Sandy sighed and answered, 'Yes lets, I'm looking forward to seeing my home for the next twelve weeks.'

'She Speaks!' Andy announced after the first sentence that Sandy finally managed to utter.

For some reason Sandy didn't take offense. Andy seemed harmless enough just a bit highly strung. Andy continued with his story, 'Now, we all start work on Monday, so I am suppose to fill you in. That was Helga's orders. How much do you know about the film?' He asked.

Sandy explained that she knew very little about the film and she only received the call from Helga a few days ago, so it was a rush to pack and leave. That started Andy on a roll, he explained to Sandy all about the film.

'This is a big blockbuster. It's called 'Under the Sea' and is a classic pirate movie, including buried treasure, but most of all it's an adventure film. It stars the pop goddess Wanda Shore in her first movie. She's the leading lady and Helga plays her mother. She wasn't too happy about that!' Andy added as a side bar, "But now she's got used to it. Guy Drovane plays Wanda's father, are you keeping up?' he asked.

'Yes, keep going, its sounds exciting. I didn't know Guy was in the film. He has been my celebrity crush since I was about sixteen.' Sandy answered.

'I know, so exciting! Well..." Andy continued, 'I cant tell you much more as I haven't read all of the script. I know that Helga and Guy's characters have travelled all over the seas to find out what has happened to their daughter and on Monday morning we will film the reunited threesome. Ok we are here,' he announced, 'Your new home for the next twelve weeks. Welcome to Beacon Hill and your Condo. It has three bedrooms and three bathrooms.'

'What am I going to do with such a big place?' Sandy asked.

'Sleep and shit in each room I guess,' he shrugged, 'I only meant shit in the bathrooms,' he explained quickly.

Sandy seeing the awkwardness in his expression laughed and told him it was ok and that she understood what he meant. Andy let out a sigh and made a quick exit. Sandy laughed out loud and proceeded to leave the car.

Andy let her in and she went straight to the large patio windows.

'Oh my goodness,' Sandy exclaimed, 'This view is Amazing!' She stood there for ages as Andy bought in her bags like a juggler in a circus, precariously and with lots of huffs and puffs, but Sandy was oblivious she just stood and watched the waves and the Caribbean sea. It was so peaceful, energising as well as magnetic.

'I've never seen such a beautiful view, its inspiring,' Sandy uttered.

Andy put the last of the bags down with gusto and took a deep sigh. 'Ok, that's it, I'm off. I will pick you up at seven o'clock for dinner, don't be late!' and he left.

Sandy heard the door shut and came out of her trance.

'What a difference from North London.' She said to herself. 'How lucky am I?'

Suddenly she heard a rap on the front door, she went over to open it and Andy was standing there holding a set of keys in his hand.

'Whoops! I forgot to say, here are your car keys. The car is under the carport and don't forget they drive on the other side of the road!'

Sandy closed the door and leant against it. This was all a bit hard to handle. North London and a steady job, her own apartment and two cats, a happy contended life. To a Condo in St Maarten, in the Caribbean, a view to die for and a job just for twelve weeks and all in just five days.

Sandy had been content with her life, she had had her relationships over the years and some even lasted longer than six months, but none of them were for life. Sandy was staunchly independent and this had always been a sticky point in every relationship. It seemed to her that most men wanted to compete with her. She was a successful independent woman and that bought problems of it's own. She had decided very young that she didn't want to be a mother. She didn't want to have the responsibility for the life of another person. Sandy had created a warm, secure unproblematic cozy life for herself. She had a large circle of friends, most of them in the same industry as herself. Television is a strange business of make believe. The whole point is making an illusion and only those in the business truly realise that, nothing is what it seems. So her closest and dearest friends are people she has met along the way, behind and in front of the camera.

Sandy very rarely went outside her comfort zone and this was now way outside of that zone. So far that she had to take a deep breath and think. With that Sandy mentally sat back and said to herself, 'what a fool, I have the chance to make a change, a change at my time of life. I have the whole world ahead of me. I have the skill and the passion and I'm bloody good at what I do. Under the Sea, here I come!' With that she started to unpack and make her new Condo her new home!

Chapter 3

Right on the dot of 7pm Sandy heard a car pull up, so she picked up her keys, left the building and locked the front door. Sandy was dressed in one of her more flamboyant outfits. It resembled a lotus flower with a large something growing out of one shoulder and she was lucky she could carry these eccentric outfits off. She had a stunning figure for her age and was quite petite at only five foot three inches tall, so she got away with it. In fact her friend Angie once described how she would 'swan into the room.' Even with the highest of heels Sandy always managed to look elegant.

Outside was the same car and driver that picked them up from the airport earlier in the day. She opened the door and got in.

'Hi I'm Alan,' said the driver with a huge smile on his face, showing his pearly white teeth, 'I hope you are all settled in.' He said in a broad Caribbean accent. To Sandy it felt like she was sitting next to Bob Marley, well if she closed her eyes it sounded like it. Sandy smiled back and announced, 'I'm all sorted and very hungry.'

Alan started driving and told her that she would be going to a local restaurant in Simpson Bay called Lee's Roadside Grill. 'It's a popular restaurant right on the lagoon.' He then went on to tell her all about the lagoon.

'Simpson Bay Lagoon is one of the largest inland lagoons in the West Indies. The border between the French and Dutch halves of the island runs across the centre of the lagoon.'

Sandy looked out of the window the whole journey and was fascinated by the vibrant Caribbean island.

'We are called the friendly Island,' Alan announced as his teeth glittered in the night light, 'You'll love it here, everyone does. You'll be hooked!' He gave a strange laugh and pulled up outside the restaurant. Sandy got out as Alan confirmed, 'I'll pick you up later. Andy will message me, have fun!'

Lee's Roadside Grill wasn't what Sandy expected. It was rather ramshackle with a temporary roof and wooden floors with cheap tables and chairs.

But the sound emanating from the small dance floor was hypnotic. There were only two singers, but together they sounded wonderful. They were singing a 1980's Stevie Wonder track and about eight couples were dancing along. Sandy was greeted by a gentleman in shorts and a t-shirt, who escorted her to a table. She followed the man to the rear of the restaurant to a long table that looked out onto the lagoon. Immediately she saw Helga with Andy sitting next to her. The rest of the table guests where all new faces. Helga stood up, waved enthusiastically and greeted her with a smile.

'Hi Sandy, I'm so pleased you're here,' Helga said happily, 'I really don't know what I would have done without you, I'm so grateful you're here. Let me introduce you to everyone. Come on sit down. Now, I know you've met Andy my PA...'

She then went around the table and introduced everyone, each of them part of the 'Helga' team. Dressers, hair, PA, yoga teacher even a bodyguard. Sandy was a little taken aback as it was only one week ago Helga was just the leading lady on a English soap opera. This team now in front of her seemed so far removed from 'The Helter Skelter' and their little team. It made Sandy wonder how long she had known about the shows closure and how long she had known about the film.

Sandy smiled and said hello to everyone and took a seat next to Andy. He passed her a menu and gushed, 'You must try the red snapper it's to die for.' Sandy nodded, accepted the menu and had a good look around the restaurant. She ordered the snapper and joined in the conversation.

Helga was a consummate leading lady. She was seated at the head of the table and rather like a judge at work she manipulated the stream of conversation, systematically bringing the conversation back to herself.

Sandy had been Helga's makeup artiste along with three or four of the other cast members for the last ten years, so every time Helga had an emotional time Sandy knew all about it. She was like a regular bar tender hearing all about Helga's bad and good days. She had been her sounding board when her first husband was sent to prison and then when her second husband was having multiple affairs. She knew all about her time in rehab, after being reliant on prescription drugs and she knew that the third husband was really gay and only married her as front for his social standing as an Actor. Helga had lived a colorful life. In fact there wasn't much Sandy didn't know about Helga's world. Sandy was stirred out of her thoughts by Helga calling, 'Sandy! Sandy. Were you surprised about the show closing down?'

Sandy joined in the conversation and told everyone how surprised she was, but also how excited she was about the upcoming project. Time went quickly and the food was delicious, the fish was superb and the company great fun. As she finished the meal she excused herself and went to find the bathroom. It was situated by the side of the kitchen and was like a wooden shack stuck on the end of a small canopy.

There were three toilets, one male and two female. Sandy went into one of the female toilets and did what she needed to do. As she came out and washed her hands she could hear whispering.

'I can't, it's impossible. You will never get away with it.' A male voice said.

Sandy stood there silently and took an enormous amount of time to wash her hands so she could stay and listen. Then another deeper voice answered, 'I've got no choice, it's got to be done tomorrow.' Sandy didn't move an inch. She didn't know what to do next, so she waited to see if they said anything else. It was silent. Sandy left the toilets and went back to the table. She sat down and tried to whisper to Andy to draw his attention. Andy didn't take the hint and just left Sandy looking slightly crazy. So she took a napkin and a pen out of her bag and wrote 'meet me outside in five minutes, I need to talk to you' and passed the note discreetly to Andy. He looked at Sandy and tried to read it secretly, but too late he was spotted by Helga.

'Passing love letters are we, I don't think your he is your type.' Helga announced, sounding like she had had one too many to drink. Andy giggled nervously as Sandy said, 'Only a shopping list, I'm afraid. Nothing elicit!'

'Boring!' said Helga a little too loudly, but this had taken Helga off the scent and nothing more was said as Andy left the table. The others where all too busy drinking and laughing to take too much notice. Sandy met Andy outside and looked very confused as he drew near.

'I'm Sorry,' Sandy said to Andy, 'I had to tell someone.'

'Tell me what?' he asked looking little panicked.

Sandy relayed the conversation she had overheard in the toilets. Andy listened and put his hand over his mouth as if to stifle a scream. Sandy realised as she finished relaying the story that maybe Andy wasn't the best person to share it with. He looked like he was going to have an apoplexy. Andy took a deep breath and said, 'Ok, they could have been talking about anything. We have no idea if you even heard it all. I'm sure it's just an innocent comment. I'm sure that it is nothing to worry about.'

'I know,' said Sandy interrupting him, 'I hope your right. I think it's better if we just forget it, I'm just being over dramatic.' She added.

Andy stood there and in a diva like panic stomped a bit and said, 'I can't forget it now you've told me and it's in my head, plus I just saw a man come out of the toilets who I'm sure served us at Bamboo Bernies. A restaurant we all went to last week. He seemed to know Helga, but she ignored him. It was all very strange, maybe it was him?'

'There is nothing we can do now, we don't know who it was directed at and even if it is a problem. It might be nothing.' Sandy said trying to soothe Andy's nerves.

'True! But...'

'No buts,' said Sandy, 'Let's just get back to our meal and forget this conversation.' She tried to go back into the restaurant, when Andy shouted, 'Don't blame me when something bad happens!'

'I won't.' Said Sandy and she made her way back to the table.

The evening wound up very soon after this as the driver came to pick Sandy up. She was exhausted and was looking forward to spending the next day getting ready for work on Monday. She stood up as the driver came to the table and said goodnight to everyone. Each person said good night in return and Andy gave a sly wink and started to bite his nails.

Sandy went straight to sleep when she got back and woke about six o'clock the next morning to the sound of two cockerels. She got up and walked to the patio doors. The view was exceptional. The sea was blue and the sun was just starting to rise, it gave the whole landscape a red hue. Sandy took some pictures then made herself some breakfast and went out on to the patio to eat it. She sat out there and contemplated how her life had changed so quickly. Last week she spent at least five or six days a week in a hot film studio working at least ten hours a day. Now she was sitting in a beautiful Condo on a Caribbean Island, being paid an extortionate amount of money for a twelve-week shoot. Life couldn't get much better.

Sandy pottered around, unpacked all her clothes and about ten o'clock there was a knock on the door. Sandy opened it to find Andy standing there in highly coloured long shorts, a white cheesecloth shirt and a baseball cap on back to front. He strutted straight in as if he owned the place and said, 'Morning! I've come to see if I can help you with anything. Helga said I'm going to be your PA today and make sure your ready to go tomorrow. So, here I am at your service.' and he took a little bow.

'Oh! Ok, I'm not used to having anyone help me, so I'm not sure what to say.' Sandy answered and thought for a while. Eventually she said, 'What

I would really like to do is see the Island, I'd like to know my way around a bit before I venture out on my own and I'd like to know where we are filming tomorrow so I know where to go. Plus I would like to see the script so I can plan ahead. I really would like to know where to shop too, if that's possible?' She garbled all in one breath.

'Anything is possible,' he answered, 'and for someone who's not used to having a helper, you sure learn fast. Ok lets think what to do first. I've got Alan our driver outside, so I think a tour of the Island is first. That one is easy! Get dressed and whatever and lets so exploring!' With that he left as dramatically as he entered.

Sandy went into her bedroom and took off her sarong and put on a bright pink kaftan, picked up a raffata bag and was ready to go!

For the next two hours Alan, Andy and Sandy drove around the Island, Alan was a perfect guide who told her all about the lovely beeches, shops, restaurants and of course the clothing optional beach.

'So, lets do lunch now.' Andy suggested and asked Alan to take them to the Little Jerusalem Restaurant in Simpson Bay for lunch.

Sandy was excited as they turned into a parking lot next to the restaurant. Little Jerusalem was made out of an old container, with a temporary roof and lots of garden furniture.

'I know what you're thinking,' said Andy, 'but I promise you this is great, you need to check out the reviews on Trip Advisor, they are all amazing!'

They were introduced to Abraham, who owned the place and they all ordered their food. Shwarma was on the menu (Or as we call it in England, Kebabs), just Shwarma in lots of ways. Curried, chicken, beef, lamb, Fallafel. It was ok as long as you wanted a Shwarma. Abraham couldn't have been any more helpful, he did his best to make everything perfect and when the meal arrived it was enormous and tasted incredible. Sandy took lots of pictures and was determined to do a picture diary of the whole twelve weeks. All three of them had something different and all of them took part of it home in a 'to go' bag.

After lunch Alan showed Sandy where they were filming and where the best supermarket was. By About three in the afternoon they got back to her place and Andy shouted from inside the car,

'Have a lovely evening and I'll see you on location at 7am. See you then! Oh and don't forget they drive on the right side!' and the car sped off.

Sandy spent a quiet evening watching American television, eating left overs and reading a book on her new purchase of an eBook reader.

Sandy was up bright and early and left her place at about half six the next morning all ready and packed with her makeup trolley (which was delivered ahead of her arrival to her Condo). The sun was up and streaming through every window. Sandy chose a bright yellow cotton jump suit and a multi coloured scarf to tie in her hair. Armed with all she needed, Sandy left her Condo and got into her car. She remembered the route and arrived exactly on time. She pulled up to a clearing near Indigo Bay beach and parked up. She saw lots of people milling around as she got her trolley out of the car. She made her way up to a gate with one solitary old security guard. He didn't look very scary, in fact he looked rather bored. Sandy approached him and he just nodded and let her in. She said, 'Good morning!' and he grunted something back and nodded again. Sandy made her way to one of the large tents erected on the beach and popped her head in. It was stuffed with clothes and she realized it was the costume department. She went to the next tent and it had a large table in the middle and a group of men talking.

'I'm looking for the makeup department.' She announced.

'Oh! You've been moved to one of the trailers over by the Beach bar.' One of them replied.

Sandy thanked them and started to walk over to the group of trailers thinking to herself that Helga, who looked like she had turned into more of a diva than she was before, had probably something to do with them moving her into an air conditioned trailer. Sandy also started to put two and two together after wondering how Helga got herself organised with this film and her crew so quickly. She made a mental note to herself to ask Andy, as she must have been working on this before they closed 'The Helter Skelter' or at least she knew what was happening. It niggled her that she didn't know before they closed the show. No gossip or warning, very suspicious. Anyway, she brushed the thoughts off and carried on looking.

She got up to the first trailer and it had 'Wanda Shaw' written on a card stuck on the door, the next one down said 'Guy Drovane' and then the third one said 'Helga Beaumont'. Sandy knocked and there is no answer, so she tried knocking again. Still nothing, so she slowly turned the handle.

The door opened and she peeped in. Looking from side to side it looked empty, no one in site. Sandy thought this a little strange as she was used to Helga always being early and teasing her on it. But never mind she thought to herself, as she walked in. The trailer had a bedroom, a large sitting room, a makeup and hair area with a mirror and a small kitchen. Sandy had a little rummage through and it was all fully stocked. There was water in the fridge along with a bottle of Champagne and Croissants. A coffee machine and snacks. In fact anything you could possibly need. Sandy started to put out all her makeup on the makeup station and was busy when the door opened and Andy bowled in.

'Morning!' He sung.

'Good morning!' Sandy replied.

'Where's Helga?' Andy asked.

'I was going to ask you that.' Sandy answered him.

'I called her at six this morning as she asked and it went straight to answer phone, so I just left a message saying wakey wakey. She is always so punctual,' he said getting worried, 'Hold on, I'll call her again.' Andy picked up his phone and dialed Helga's number.

'Nope, straight to answer phone again. That's strange, let me ask if anyone has seen her,' he said sounding a little panicky as opened the trailer door and left. Seconds later he returned.

'Oh NO! Sandy, remember last night?' Andy gasped as he turned back to talk to her. 'What you heard, maybe it was Helga they were after, now I am really worried.'

'I'm sure she is fine.' Sandy said, 'Just go ask around, I'm sure someone knows.' She said reassuringly as Andy left.

Sandy carried on with her unpacking. She got out a small bowl and went to the kitchen to fill it with water. Nothing happened. No water came out of the tap, so she looked around to find the bathroom door and just as she was about to turn the handle the trailer door opened. In walked Andy again with a worried look on his face.

'No one has seen her!' he told Sandy as he walked in, 'I'm worried. She is normally so punctual. I don't like it, something must have happened to her, I am sure of it.'

At that precise moment Sandy opened the bathroom door and as she did the lifeless body of Helga dropped on to the floor with one almighty thud. Her head was covered with blood and she was not breathing. Andy screamed and jumped backwards with hands flying everywhere as Sandy uttered under her breath, 'Well something has definitely happened to her.' It was a smart remark to hide the total astonishment of finding a dead body and not just any dead body, but the body of someone she had worked with for years. Sandy wanted to scream, she wanted to scream really loudly and cry but her survival instinct kicked in and although her first urge was to fall apart, she took a deep breath and took charge of the situation. Andy became hysterical.

'What are we going to do?' He screamed and stamped as one person after another tried to get in to the trailer after hearing the screams, to see what was going on. There were lots of shouts of 'what's wrong?' and lots more screaming, in fact it turned into one humongous panic until Sandy took control and asked loudly for the Director to call the police and everyone to get out as they could be disturbing the evidence. She pushed Andy out and they both left the trailer, leaving the body of Helga inside.

Sandy's mind was in a whirl, this wasn't good, not only because it might have been murder, but her mind was thinking, 'shit what am I going to do now?' plus after hearing the strange conversation last night, it made her think, should she have told someone other than Andy. All these thoughts were whirring through her mind when she saw that David the Director was walking towards her. Everyone had left the trailer so that when the police arrived, they could do their job.

'Are you Ok? I heard you found the body, I mean Helga?' David said, as he got nearer. 'I've called the police, but I don't think they will get here very soon. It doesn't work the same out here in the Caribbean. I can't believe our luck. I've no idea how we are going to deal with this. The last thing I want to do is stop production, it will coast us millions. I'll have to get hold of Mark our Producer. Man! This is terrible.' he added all in one breath, 'I can't believe anyone would want to harm her.' He added as an after thought.

'Who's going to tell her Family? Her daughter?' Sandy whispered.

'Don't worry, we will make sure everything is dealt with.' David answered with honesty. Then he walked of muttering to himself. As he walked away his mobile phone rang. It was the police calling him back.

Andy walked towards her, with tears in his eyes, 'I can't believe it, who would harm Helga? Sandy what are we going to do?' he gasped as he sat down on a chair.

Sandy looked at Andy sitting on the chair weeping and rocking to and fro.

'Andy.' She called to him rather loudly. 'We've got to be strong, she would have wanted that. Now you've got lots to deal with, we are all going to need you. You are the one who knew most about Helga and the police will want to talk to you, and me!' she told him gently.

Andy looked up at Sandy and with puppy dog eyes.

'Me?' he said really quietly, 'What do I know?' he added.

'Her last whereabouts firstly and everything else about her. This first hour after finding a body is called The Golden Hour and it's when the police need to find out as much as possible to be able to solve it as quickly as possible, but first I think we need to consider what this could mean to us.' Sandy said.

'I don't understand.' He answered.

Sandy explained that with Helga not around they will no longer be needed and that if they play it right they could keep their jobs.

'How can we do that?' Andy said rather puzzled.

'I have an idea, I'll explain later. For now I think we need to see what's happening and wait for the police.'

Chapter 4

It took about two hours for the police to arrive and do the necessary investigative procedures. They set up a command centre in one of the large tents that Sandy first looked in when she arrived at the location. They asked each person to stay where they were on the set to be interviewed. Andy was called in first and was in there for about forty minutes. When he walked out his eyes where looking down and he looked distraught.

'They think I did it!' he told sandy rather loudly between his sobs.

'Are you sure?' Sandy replied.

'It was horrible. They accused me of terrible things. I'm Helga's biggest fan and they didn't believe me,' he told her disjointedly.

Sandy thought for a minute as Andy sobbed silently and then she said, 'Andy, I think that's just what they do. They do it to try and get the right person to admit it. What's strange is at the moment no one has even confirmed it's murder, she could have died of natural causes. She could have had a heart attack or something. They came and took Helga away about ten minutes ago and they have taped off the trailer.'

Andy stopped sobbing and just looked at Sandy.

'Oh my goodness, that's so true, she might not have been murdered!' Andy said with a glint in his eye.

At that point a policeman came out of the tent and called Sandy in. Sandy followed him into the tent and inside there were another three policeman. All Male. A desk a table and about six chairs. She was asked to sit on one side of the table. One of the policemen sat at the desk, one on the other side of the table and one stood behind. It felt intimidating, obviously exactly what they wanted. Her interrogator was a white man, dressed in a white shirt and beige trousers. The other two policemen looked like locals. His shirt had an emblem on it and she guessed it was the St Maarten flag. Nothing was said for a while whilst he read through some paperwork. Then he looked up and started speaking.

'Hello Miss Bernstein. My Name is Hans Larrs and I am the Chief of Police here in St Marten,' he said with a slight European accent. Probably Dutch she thought, as this was a Dutch Island.

'I'm sorry your first visit to the Island has been disrupted by this terrible incident.'

Sandy just nodded and listened, wondering how he knew it was her first visit and waited for his first question.

'I'm sorry to have to ask you some questions, but as you can imagine we need to work out what has happened.'

'Was she murdered?' Sandy asked bluntly.

'We are not sure at the moment, we need to wait for the *lijkschouwer* I mean Coroner to tell us for certain. So, for now we are just asking everyone the same questions so we can get as much information together as we can. May I ask you when was the last time you spoke to Helga?'

Sandy explained about how they all went out for dinner on Saturday night and the last time she spoke with her was as they left the restaurant. She didn't, however, mention about the strange conversation she overheard in the toilet.

'Thank you,' the policeman answered, 'I know you have known Helga for a long time, is there anyone you could think of, anyone who would want to harm her or has any reason to see her dead.'

Before she had time to answer the Officer's mobile phone rang and she sat there as he answered it. He spoke in a foreign language and seemed to ask a lot of questions, although she wasn't sure, as she didn't understand a word of it. He put the phone down and said something to the other officers. They got up and left as he apologised, 'I'm sorry, we are going to have to leave it there, please don't leave the Island as I will be asking you some more questions along with the rest of the company.'

Then he left, leaving Sandy bemused and very glad she didn't have to say anymore. She got up and made her way out of the tent. Andy was waiting outside and looked like he had been pacing.

'What did they say? What did they ask you? Why have they left?' He quizzed.

'That's a lot of questions all in one breath.' Sandy replied.

'It's important, did they ask you about me?' He asked frantically.

'No.' Sandy replied. 'We didn't talk about you at all.'

She then went on to tell him everything the Chief of Police said, leaving nothing out.

'Oh!' said Andy, 'That's rather disappointing, so its only me they suspect then?'

Sandy went on to tell him that she asked if Helga had been murdered and they had said they were not sure of anything at the moment. Then she added about the call and then they left.

'Oh!' Andy said again, 'What are we going to do now?'

Sandy thought for a while and then said, 'I think we need to get involved.'

'How?' Asked Andy.

'If we manage to find out who killed her, because I do think she was killed, then the production team are going to be so thankful, they may not send us home and at the moment my priority is this job. I really don't want to lose it and as I came out here as Helga's makeup Artiste and she's, well, not here, I am redundant and we can't have that. I don't know about you but in the two days I've been here I've already fallen in love with the Island and I don't want to go home.'

'Ditto!' Andy added, 'but, how can we solve a murder?'

'I'm not sure yet, but with your skills and mine, we must be able to do this,' she told him.

Andy looked troubled and asked, 'Where do we even start?'

Sandy replied, 'We can't do anything or say too much here, let's see what happens for the rest of the day and meet up later and set up a plan. The police are not going to let everyone go until they have spoken to everyone I'm guessing and if that call was about Helga, then we need to sit tight and just see what happens. I do need to talk to David though or at least someone who can give us assurances that we still have a job. If I can get some assurance that they will keep us here for a while, it will give us some time to start investigating.'

Andy looked troubled, but just nodded slowly.

Sandy smiled and said to him, 'It will be fine, I'm sure we' will make a good team and between us we will find out what happened.'

'I wish I had your confidence.' Andy replied.

Most of the rest of the day was taken up with sitting around gossiping and waiting for the police or David the Director to say something. By about one that afternoon the police returned and entered the tent they had all gathered in. Paul Ferris the Assistant Director called quiet and made an announcement.

'The police have now confirmed that Helga was murdered and they wish to speak to everybody. Once you have spoken to them you will be free to go. We will have one day dark and then on Wednesday we will start filming again.'

He came over to Sandy and Andy and said, 'The police said you two can go as they have asked you all they need.'

Sandy took this opportunity to put her plan into action.

'I'm not sure if you can help, but with Helga not being here, we wondered if there was anything else we can help with. Would we be need to help with whomever takes over?'

Paul thought for a while and then made a call on his mobile, walking away as he spoke to someone. In less than a minute he came back and said, 'We would like you to do the same role for whomever takes over the part. It seems silly to bring in a new team when you two are already here, so take it as carry on as if nothing had happened.' With that he walked away and Andy piped up with, 'Nothing has happened, is he joking, there has been a bloody murder. We've lost Helga! Nothing has happened!' he managed to splutter, 'Bloody hell!' He added and stomped off.

Sandy followed Andy and calmed him down and reminded him that she had just secured their job and that was very good news. Now she needed to work out how she was going to find out if the coroner had recorded a cause of death. This had to be the priority as it was no use starting to ask too many questions if it was natural causes. Sandy thought to herself 'there was an awful lot of blood on Helga's face, when she fell out of the bathroom. I can't believe that was from anything natural'.

Andy sobbed again loudly and that bought Sandy back to the present as she turned to Andy and said, 'I need your help. I need you to be my spy.'

Andy stopped sobbing instantly and brightened up.

'A Spy?' He repeated. 'What do you need me to do?'

Sandy asked Andy if he would just mingle around the crew and ask some questions, but to be careful not to sound too over the top, which might prove hard for the exuberant Andy,

and then meet her at her Condo when he finished. Andy saluted Sandy and said, 'Ok! I'm off!' He then whispered, 'Detective Andy at your service!'

As he left and walked over to some of the crew Sandy realised her bag with her car keys were still inside Helga's trailer. She wasn't sure what to do. She guessed that it might be impossible to get in the trailer as it was a murder scene, but what the heck. She had to try otherwise she was in shit street. She wasn't going anywhere.

She made her way out of the tent and over to the trailer.

It was very quiet, there was no one walking around and all she could hear was the sound of the sea and a plane flying overhead. She waked behind the three tents, one was costume, one was the canteen and a meeting room where everyone was stationed at the moment and another one for the Director and his crew. Behind those tents were the trailers. First was Wanda's the leading lady. She was an established pop singer who wanted to move away from that scene and this was her first film. The next trailer belonged to Mark Morris, he was playing the baddy in the film. Sandy had never met him and he wasn't on set this morning, neither had Wanda. The following trailer belonged to Guy her childhood crush and then Helga's. As she got up close to Helga's trailer she saw that nothing and changed. There wasn't a long trail of police tape round it as she has suspected. It was just as she had left it, minus the dead body of course. Maybe they do things here differently, she thought to herself.

Sandy walked up, looked around either side of her and once again turned the handle slowly just like she had down a few hours ago. It opened and she looked in. Nothing had changed at all. It looked exactly as she entered it a few hours before. Sandy saw her bag on the table and stepped into the trailer. As she reached for her bag, she saw that maybe it wasn't just as she left it. There was a dark stain on the floor outside the bathroom door so she Just reached for her bag and as she did she heard a voice behind her.

'What yuh doin?' a deep voice said sternly from the doorway with Caribbean drawl. She turned round to see a local policeman standing at the door.

'I just came to get my bag.' she answered sweetly.

'Yuh shud'nt be doin dat!' he said.

'I'm leaving now. I just needed my bag and car keys,' she added.

'Dis is a murder scene,' he added.

Sandy had to make a quick decision and decided to play the sweet innocent.

'I haven't touched anything, I promise,' she told him.

The man looked her up and down with a suspicious gleam in his eye and didn't say anything for at least ten seconds. Sandy just stood there in silence too.

'Ok, you can go Miss Sandy,' he added.

Sandy picked up her bag and fled. She could hear the policeman, sniggering behind her.

Sandy went straight back to her car and made her way back to her condo, stopping for some groceries on the way. She arrived home and opened up, walked in and once again, leant up against the door. Something she had done a lot of lately. She took a deep sigh, stripped off her clothes and jumped into the shower. Just as she got out she heard a tap on the front door. Thinking it was Andy she wrapped a towel round her head and another round her body and opened the door. There wasn't anyone there. Sandy looked either way down the road and then on the floor. On the step was a brown envelope. She picked it up and looked both ways down the road to see if she could see who left it and went back inside.

For a short while she just sat down and looked at the large envelope without opening it. All of sudden the door just opened and Andy walked in saying, 'I'm back!' rather loudly.

Sandy wondered how he got in just a he said, 'You left the door open so I let myself in.' Sandy was still holding the envelope, which caught Andy's eye. 'What's that?' he asked.

Sandy explained how it was just left by the front door and that she wasn't sure if she should open it.

Andy reassured her that it might not be anything suspicious as he had ordered a copy of the script for her and it was probably that.

Sandy decided to get dressed before opening the envelope, she left Andy wanting to know what was inside and promised him she wouldn't be long.

Andy looked relived when sandy started to open the envelope. She pulled out the contents and was stunned, it wasn't the script at all it was a photo. A photo of Helga in the arms of Guy Trovane!

'Oh shit!' said Andy as he saw the picture, 'That aint no script.'

Chapter 5

'Nope!' said Andy, 'That sure aint no script, I wonder who dropped it off!' he added.

'Someone is trying to tell us something, but who and what, and do they have something to do with the murder or not?' Sandy said out loud, but more thinking to herself.

'That's a lots of questions.' Andy said.

'Yep and I wonder who took the picture?' Sandy said as she turned over the photo.

They both saw a label and Andy started to get excited, 'Look, Look it says Phillip's photo's, Front Street, Phillipsburg. I know where that is, we could go and find out who had it printed! Oh No! That now makes sense!' Andy added. He went on to tell Sandy that he did just as he was asked and tried to get some gossip from the other cast and crew. It seems that Helga was the only actor on set as Wanda and Mark were not due in that day and Guy hadn't arrived. When he did arrive they asked him to leave as it was after they had found Helga's body. The police spoke to him and let him go.

Then Andy chatted to some of the crew, lighting, camera, electrical, grips etc... He spoke to lots of them, pretending to be a bit of a gossip, but none of them seemed to know anything. He then went over and spoke to some of the people in the costume department. They were a bit like those in the makeup department, the actors seemed to tell them everything and they tended to confide in them too. They were much more open and loved to gossip about everyone. One of the ladies, called Amie, pulled him aside and said she knew what had been going on between Guy and Helga .

Sandy said, 'Go on! What did she say?' wanting to know more. Andy went on to say that Amie knew Guy and Helga had been having an affair for over fifteen years off and on, but Guy's wife seemed to ignore the fact that her husband played away. The two of them sat and thought about this information.

'Maybe Guy's wife is the murderer.' Sandy suggested, 'She has got motive and opportunity, but...' she said as she was thinking out loud. 'We need to find out how Helga died, until we find out that we can't move on. It's no good finding out any more until we know the facts.' Sandy said.

As soon as she finished the sentence there was a knock at the door. They both turned round suddenly as if it was a sign.

Andy whispered, 'Who's that?'

Sandy answered, 'I can't see through doors, you'll have to open it to see.'

'It's your house!'

'Oh yes!' she answered and got up to see who was there. She opened the door to find the Chief of Police standing there.

She asked him if he wanted to come in and he followed her into the Condo. Sandy offered him a seat and they all sat and waited to see what he said.

He started off by saying that he was glad they were both there, as he wanted to speak with the two of them. He then said that he needed their help. Sandy and Andy looked stunned and Sandy asked, 'How can we help?'

'First, please call me Lucas, I have a feeling we are going to be working closely together for a while so if you don't mind I would like to keep this personal, if you don't mind me calling you both by your first names.' He said all of this in his broken English.

Sandy and Andy just nodded and waited to hear more. Lucas continued to say that he thought the two of them were in a perfect position to find out more about what happened to Helga from the inside. At that comment Andy went to say something and Sandy kicked him in the shin. Instead of taking the hint Andy let out a yelp as Sandy said, 'We would love to help!' hoping to cover up what Andy might say next. Lucas carried on and told the both of them that he still wasn't sure how Helga had died. Sandy and Andy waited with baited breath to hear what they needed to carry on their own personal enquires.

'And you can't tell us anything?' Sandy asked Lucas.

Lucas carried on to say that he wanted to know first if they were prepared to work with him and that no one was to know that this was so. With the exception of Lars and Hans his two Sergeants. 'Apart from those two no one else will know our plan. That's the safest way to find our killer!'

'What do we need to do?' Andy asked.

'Firstly I need to be in contact with both of you, so here is a cell phone that's set up to call me. Please be careful, who ever this is has killed once so killing again could be possible. I need you to stay safe. Secondly your first task is to ask questions, I need to find out all the gossip and...'

Andy went to butt in and say that he had done that already until he saw Sandy's look and stopped short.

Sandy took over and said, 'No Problem, I'm sure we can do this and it's important to us that we find out what happened to Helga so if we can help any way we are up for it.'

'Yep me too!' added Andy.

Lucas didn't stay much longer, they arranged to keep in contact and get as much info as possible and he agreed to let them know more as and when he finds details out. As soon as he was gone Andy said, 'I'm confused. Why didn't we tell him what we have find out already and about the envelope?'

Sandy told him that if they admitted they had this information already, he would wonder what they had been doing and why they hadn't told him before. It looked suspicious and he may not want to work with them if he doesn't trust them.

'Andy, we need to get organised and I'll need your help. We need to convert my second bedroom. We need a murder investigation board, so we can write up clues, add suspects etc... Also, I need you to get a notebook and keep notes of what we have found out so far and everything that happens from now on. Can you do that?' Sandy asked.

'Andy the PA at your service,' replied Andy.

'Can you get a shopping list ready of things to buy for me? First is a white board or two pin boards. Plenty of white board pens, pins, sticky notes and a printer/scanner and I'll add anything as I think of it.'

Andy was eager and happy to go shopping, he got up and told Sandy he will be back soon with everything she needed and strolled out of the Condo.

Sandy was glad to be alone. It and been a very stressful day so far and a little peace and quiet was just what the doctor ordered. She took out her eBook reader and went out onto the porch and started to read. She paused and looked at the magical view in front of her and pondered who could hate a human being so much that they would want to kill someone. It was so far out of Sandy's spectrum, that she found it impossible to fathom. It was at that point Sandy wondered how her cats were. It's funny at times like this that you need to feel love from a trusted pet. Sandy made a mental note to check out how Alphaba and Glinda were as soon as possible.

She had only been out there about ten minutes before she fell fast asleep. She woke up to the sound of, 'Ooo hoo, wakey wakey!' Andy was cooing over her. Sandy opened her eyes and adjusted to the light. 'Oh you're back,' she said.

Andy explained that he got everything that was on the list and that he had moved the furniture in the second bedroom and put up two large white boards.

'Come and see our new investigating room, It's all ready.'

Sandy got up and followed Andy into the room. He had done an amazing job. There were two large white boards, lots of notebooks, and pens and stuff, they could now get organised properly. Sandy turned to Andy and said, 'I don't think there is much we can do today, but we can go to the print shop tomorrow and see who ordered the photo's. So if you could pick me up at nine in the morning we can go together and start of our official investigation.'

'Ok boss!' Andy answered and prepared to leave.

Sandy said goodbye and went back into her special room to start work on the murder of Helga Beaumont.

The next morning at precisely 9am two things happened, there was a knock on the door and the mobile phone rang.

Sandy picked up the phone and answered it at the same time as opening the front door.

'Hello.' She said to the person on the phone, knowing very well that it was Lucas, as he was the only person that knew that number. She was holding the phone under her chin leaving her hands free to open the door. Andy walked in and acknowledged she was on the phone, he also gave her a rather strange look up and down.

Sandy had chosen to wear one of her more exotic outfits, of multicolored harem pants and a cheesecloth white shirt.

'Hi Lucas.' She answered to the caller as well as using her hand to ask Andy to come in. Andy could only hear one side of the conversation, but tried to put two and two together. He got fed up of trying and walked into the 'Murder Room" as he had named it. Now on the wall was a picture of Helga in the centre of one board. A line had been drawn down and then the picture of Guy and Helga stuck there. Andy turned round just as Sandy walked into the room. She told him that Lucas asked them if they would start today finding out as much as they could.

'What are we going to do?' Andy asked.

Sandy explained that they could use some of the info they had already acquired to keep him happy and then said that she had got his email address, so she could email him at the end of the day. So they got ready to leave and visit Phillip's Photo's.

'Am I driving?' Sandy asked.

'Yep!' said Andy, 'I'm not driving out here, first it's the other side of the road and second, they are all crazy. Especially those buses that stop wherever they want. I think I would die if I had to drive here. I got a taxi here this morning.'

Sandy smiled as she picked up her car keys and they made their way outside.

It was about a twenty-minute drive from where Sandy was staying, over a very steep hill with amazing views over the Caribbean Sea to Philipsburg. They decided to stop at the top of the hill to take some pictures. It was the perfect spot, full of tourists that come off of the cruise boats to see the Island.

'St Maarten is a very busy cruise port, they're can be up to six or seven boats in dock each day. That means the capital, Phillipsburg, can get an influx of over 25,000 people all in one day,' informed Andy. The view was breathtaking and in the distance you could see the Island of Saba and the sea was a deep shade of blue and seemed to have an air of stillness, even though they were actually on the side of a very busy road. Sandy didn't want to move, but just stay there and watch for hours, but Andy reminded her they were on a mission. So she got back in to the car and drove off.

The roads were very busy and Sandy used the drive to find out more about Andy. He was thirty-two years old and he had grown up in a small town in Essex called Great Dunmow, about five miles from Stansted airport. He was always quite a character, outgoing and confident and this caused many dilemmas as a child. He was always seen as the class clown and that caused problems with the teachers. He was forever being given detentions and called in to see the Head of Year and told he must conform and not cause problems. This didn't go down well with Andy or his supportive parents. Why would you ask a child to conform and not give them the chance to grow and be nurtured? Andy was also rather effeminate and that was another whole big problem. He would be called names and teased and set upon by bullies. Andy's goal was just to get through each day at a time.

His saving grace was the local drama group. They didn't tease him they just included him. It was from the head of the group that he got the chance to be a Personal Assistant for his first client. At the age of twenty-one, when he had finished a degree in Media, he was offered a chance to interview to PA for one of the Directors friends. He got the job and he was in his element, so he left Essex and moved to Canary Wharf. Andy was a natural organiser and he loved his job. He worked for his first client until she fell pregnant and then he was traded over to her friend and from there he was always working. This gig with Helga was really short lived. Andy only started working for her about two months ago and she was up to date the most difficult client he had ever worked with. She was always annoyingly late, very disorganised and often changed her mind. All of this contributed to her being named privately as the 'Princess.'

Andy directed Sandy to Front Street as he was checking the number to see if he could work out where the store they were looking for was.

'There it is!' Andy shouted, 'Well I think it is,' he added.

Sandy skidded to a halt and turned the car onto the shop front. Andy held on tight and said, 'Wooohhhh that was close.'

Sandy smiled as she realised she had scared Andy just a little. Sandy loved to drive, it was a hobby of hers. She had done many of those days at the track where she had driven all types of racing and restive cars. She felt very safe in the car, but realised that maybe her passengers didn't feel quite so safe. She turned off the engine as Andy got out of the car. Sandy called him back with, 'Andy let's just chat about how we are going to tackle this.'

Andy got back in as Sandy said, 'I think we need to take this carefully, they may not want to divulge the info, we need to think how we are going to do this.'

They chatted away and made a plan and both got out and went into the shop. Andy opened the door and let Sandy in first. The shop was full of large televisions, computers and mobile phones. Every possible space in the long thin shop was full. St Maarten is tax and duty free, so all the cruise visitors flock in to buy their electrical goods. It was busy too in the shop with lots of people milling around. Sandy looked out of the window and noticed a man on the opposite side of the road, just leaning on his car watching them. She shrugged it off as there were so many people mingling about, that she thought she was being paranoid.

Sandy looked up and saw a small sign over the top of a door, it said 'Phillips Photo's'. She nudged Andy and they both made their way forward where they could see through to a glass counter and a man standing behind it. It was a busy space with lots of beautiful pictures on all the walls. They walked in and heard 'Good morning. Can I help you?' from a Dutch accent.

Sandy was holding the original photo, as it was a scanned copy she had put on the wall back at the Condo.

'I wonder if you can help? We are working with The Chief of Police here on the Island and he has sent us to find out a bit of information about this photo.' Sandy passed over the photo. The man looked at the back and put it down and said, 'How can I help?'

'We are looking for some information on the person that came in to purchase the picture, we are on a murder investigation and we need to rule this person from our inquiries.'

The man looked at both of them and then went over to another desk and picked up a large notebook. He looked up the number on the back of the photo and wrote something on a piece of paper. He handed it to Sandy and said, 'Is this about the murder on the film set?' It seemed he wanted to find out the gossip. Sandy put the note in her handbag as Andy said to the man, 'I'm so sorry we can't confirm anything, but just to say you are really helping our investigation. Thank you so much.'

Andy shook the man's hand and they both left without looking at the note. Somehow it didn't seem right and they walked through the main store and got back in to the car.

'Well! Let's read it.' Andy enthused.

Sandy took out the note but waited to open it.

'Are you just trying to annoy me?' Andy shouted. 'Come on who is it?'

Sandy read what was on the note but secretly so Andy couldn't see it and said, 'Well you are not going to believe this.'

'What? I can't take the suspense, come on!'

Sandy was enjoying teasing Andy, but knew it was time to share, 'It says Mrs Trovane,' she announced.

'Blimey!' Andy added, 'I didn't expect that. So have we found our Murderer?'

'No,' said Sandy, 'There are a lot more details to find out yet. Who dropped this off, what did Mrs Drovane do when she got this printed and, I just thought of something! Lucas didn't tell us how Helga was killed, just that it was confirmed she was murdered.'

'Do you think he will tell you?' Andy asked.

'There is only one way to find out, I'll have to call him.' Sandy answered. Sandy made the call and wasn't surprised when Lucas told her that he wasn't allowed to tell her any more details accept that she was dead for about an hour before Sandy found the body. Sandy told him that they were going to find out what they can that day and that she would report back to him as soon as they knew anything, thinking that would keep him off their backs for a while. It's time to work out our next step.

'Cor, there's a lot more to this investigating business than I first thought,' said Andy.

'Yep,' said Sandy, 'We are only just touching the surface, I think there is a lot more we are going to find out before we find our killer.'

Chapter 6

They sat in the car and came up with a plan. Andy, like all the actor's PA's received a list of everyone's details on the set, so he sent a text to Nancy, Guy's wife, to ask if she fancied meeting up for lunch, as he has come into some information about Helga's death that she might find interesting. He had met her a few times so contacting her wasn't too strange. Although he bet she was only coming because she was intrigued or because she was the murderer and she wanted to know how much they knew. Either way it didn't matter. They could either strike her off the list or get her arrested. Within five minutes she had replied and they arranged to meet up for lunch at midday that day at Mark's Place, a local restaurant on the way back from Phillipsburg, in the car park of a large supermarket.

As they had a few hours to spare, Andy suggested they went to Front Street and shopped.

'Shopping!' Sandy repeated, 'Perfect!'

They parked the car in the little car park at the end of the back street. Andy took Sandy to the local market where you could buy lots of local Caribbean trinkets. Sandy loved it. She bought herself lots of Caribbean dresses, loud and colorful, just her style.

Suddenly she looked up from the market stall she was rummaging through and thought she saw the same face as the one at the photo shop, but shrugged it off. She had a good look round and couldn't see anyone that looked like the same man. She was going to say something to Andy and then thought better of it as she really didn't have anything to say, just a feeling of being watched.

Time seemed to speed by and it was time to leave to meet up with Nancy. They got back into the car and Sandy drove to the restaurant. They arrived just before noon and walked into Mark's Place and sat at a table. It was a strange place. It looked like a temporary building that had been here for years. It had wooden tables and chairs and lots of signs promoting their most popular dishes. A waitress came over and gave them a menu. Andy at once said, 'I'm starving and their ribs are to die for!'

They ordered some drinks and decided to wait for Nancy before ordering lunch. As soon as the drinks arrived so did a large black Hummer. It pulled up outside the restaurant and out stepped a lady. She was dressed from head to toe in beige. A beige trouser suit. Her hair was perfect and huge and not a hair out of place. She reminded Sandy of an American First Lady. She walked into the restaurant with her head held high and looked around. Andy stood up and waved as Nancy saw him and walked over.

'Hi Nancy,' he said in a friendly voice.

'What is this all about?' Nancy said with anger.

Sandy noticed that the black Hummer was still in the car park, with the driver standing outside, watching in. She turned back as Andy said, 'Please sit down and join us.'

'Who's is this?' Nancy asked rather rudely.

'This is Sandy and she is, or was, Helga's makeup artiste.' Andy answered.

Nancy sat down and said, 'I have no idea why you two have asked me here.'

Andy gave Nancy a menu and she handed it back saying, 'I'm not hungry, just get on with what you've got to say!'

Sandy then butted in and said, 'Hi Nancy, I've known Helga for a very long time now and I was devastated to find her.' She took a breath as if she was stopping a sob.

Andy smiled and then changed back to his serious face.

'Please accept our apologies for the very vague text, but we really needed to speak with you in private. The last thing we wanted was for the police to find out what we did, so please don't worry, we are on your side.'

Nancy's tough face, warmed a little as Andy raised his eyebrow. Sandy carried on making Nancy warm to her. She then went on to tell Nancy how a brown envelope was left at her door and when she opened it... Sandy stopped as she saw Nancy's eyes rise as if she knew what was in the envelope. She didn't need to say anything it was obvious.

'It's Ok. I know what was in there,' Nancy said, 'Although I have no idea who the hell got hold of it, but if your thinking I killed Helga you are way off the mark.' She gave a strange small laugh that sounded slightly evil. Nancy went on to explain that she found out what her husband had been up to about two weeks ago. She had asked her driver to follow him and take pictures. It wasn't until she got to the island she found someone to print the pictures. Both sandy and Andy let her carry on and tell her story.

Nancy went on to say, 'What I'm about to tell you must stay between us.'

Both Sandy and Andy nodded in agreement.

Nancy admitted that she took the photos to Guy and asked him to explain. He admitted that he had been seeing her for a while, but now it was over. Nancy then took a moment and started again. 'We spoke at length and we decided to make it work. We've been married now for eighteen years and you don't throw that away. We have both made mistakes but we decided to work through it. So I'm afraid you've got it wrong, I am not your killer. You need to look elsewhere and if you don't mind I would like that photo back.'

Andy stopped Sandy handing over the envelope by putting his hand on it and saying, 'I still have a couple of questions. Where were you this morning at about 6am?'

Nancy gave strange sort of laugh and said, 'that is an easy one Andy. Guy and I were in hospital on the French side. Go there and you'll find out exactly where we were.'

'That's convenient!' Andy said under his breath.

Sandy then butted in and asked, 'Would you mind sharing with us why you were at the hospital just so we can, you know, substantiate your story.'

'I'm not sure who turned you to the police force,' she said in a rather bitchy way.

'Well...' Andy was just about to spill the beans until Sandy stopped him and said, 'You must remember that we both have Helga's best interest at heart.'

'If I tell you, you must swear not to repeat it to anyone, the last thing we need at the moment is paparazzi tuning in for a story.'

'Of Course.' They both said in unison.

Nancy opened her handbag, took out a lipstick and mirror and re-applied the colour to her lips. Sandy and Andy looked on and waited with baited breath. She put the lipstick back in to her bag

From Makeup to Murder

slowly and took out a couple pieces of paper and handed them over to Sandy. Sandy could see that it was a prescription and a hospital report sheet. Looking at the report it said that Guy Drovane was cut out of a pair of handcuffs that were too tight on his wrists at 4am that morning. Sandy handed back the papers and Nancy said, 'Satisfied?' She got up, brushed down her trouser suit, picked up her bag and left.

Andy waited until she was a safe distance away and asked, 'What the hell was on that report?'

'Let's just say, I know she wasn't the murderer as she was with her husband and he was, shall we say, busy!' Sandy answered.

'You're not going to tell me, are you?' Andy asked.

'Nope, lets order lunch.' Sandy suggested.

Andy realised she wasn't going to spill the beans, so the next important task was to eat! They started on their food when Andy asked, 'Who dropped that envelope then?'

'I'm guessing it was Nancy's driver, he must have been suspicious and wanted to give us a lead,' Sandy answered.

Sandy and Andy enjoyed their lunch and chatted about their next steps. Sandy said she was going to email Lucas all about Nancy and Guy, so they can count them out. At least that would show that they have been doing something.

They finished their food and made their way back to Sandy's Condo. When they got back they removed the picture and info about Nancy from the investigation room and chatted about what to do next.

'I am meeting some of the PA's and crew tonight for dinner, do you want to come with? At least you'll get a chance to gossip with all of them?' Andy offered.

Sandy jumped at the chance and they arranged to meet up later. Andy said his driver would pick her up at seven o'clock and that they were going out of an Indian meal.

'Perfect,' said Sandy, 'I'll enjoy gossiping with everyone.'

With that Andy left and Sandy was once again alone and able to relax.

She spent some time researching as much as she could about the crew, producers and directors on the production, giving herself some background information on as many people as possible. About five o'clock she received a text from Andy it read:

'I think we shouldn't say we are working for the police tonight, that could stop them talking xxxx.'

Sandy smiled as she had already realised that was the best course of action. She answered with, 'Agreed!'

At exactly seven o'clock a car hooted and Sandy locked up and left. Andy was waving as she walked towards the car. He looked very excited about something. Sandy opened the car door as Andy said, 'You won't believe it!' enthusiastically.

'Won't believe what?' Sandy asked.

Andy went on to say that he heard from one of the costume designers that Wanda Shore had been for a clothes fitting today and she said to him that she was pleased Helga's dead! 'Can you believe it?' he added.

Sandy put on her seat belt and thought about the comment. Whilst she was still contemplating Andy spoke up again.

'Don't you think that's weird? Why would you even admit that, especially to a stranger,' he added.

'I think she is lonely. She obviously hasn't got anyone to talk to if the only one she confides in is a costume designer. How sad, but more importantly, why is she glad Helga's dead? That's what I would like to know, is he coming with us tonight this designer?'

Andy said he was along with everyone else from the costume department and then Wanda's PA as well as Mark's PA.

Sandy was excited as they drove off to meet everyone; it was only down the road so it didn't take long. They parked up in the car park and got out of the car. Sandy could see a large group of people all drinking and chatting. They walked over to the table and Andy introduced her to everyone. There was Abi from the costume department, Stuart, Wanda's Makeup Artiste, Mark a Camera Man, Linda, Mark's PA, Georgia who is in charge of all the set catering, Sam the Locations Director, Daisy, Wanda's Dresser, Chris, Wanda's PA and Tom, Wanda's security guard.

She immediately felt a kinship with Stuart, Wanda's makeup artiste and guessed they were going to be friends.

It was difficult to remember everyone's names. She was sat between Stuart and the costume departments Abi. It was a lovely warm evening and everyone seemed jolly and the atmosphere was lighthearted. It was difficult to hear what everyone was saying, as everyone was chatting away. Both Abi and Stuart told her they were devastated at the sad news of Helga's murder. Sandy thanked them and they all carried on chatting. Everyone ordered and as they were waiting Andy asked a question to the whole table.

'So guy's...' he said to get everyone's attention, 'Who do you think did it?' He said the words boldly.

Sandy took an intake of breath and stifled a giggle. Luckily no one was looking her way, everyone was looking at him dumb founded at his straightforwardness. Sandy just thought to herself that 'there's nothing like honesty' and waited for someone to say something. First to speak was Tom, he said in his gruff voice, 'Bloody hell, who knows, she wasn't everyone favorite person.'

'I know,' agreed Abi, 'She was bloody rude to me on Sunday when she came for a fitting.'

'What did she do?' Andy asked.

Abi explained that on Sunday Helga was due to be fitted for some of her costumes at two o'clock, but she didn't turn up until three and she came straight in and said, I hope this isn't going to take long. 'Bloody rude if you ask me, I'm not surprised she made enemies but to be murdered well that some kind of hatred. I'm not sure I know anyone who capable of that,' she added.

Everyone seemed then to have something to say and added their story. It seemed that although Helga had only arrived a few days before her death she had made enemies, but none of the stories added up to pure hatred, just bloody rude or annoyance. This did seem a little strange to Sandy as she had known her a long time and it seemed like they were talking about a different person, not the woman she had been looking after for so long. That in it's self seemed to be clue. She wondered why she had changed her attitude since she got here and she made a mental note to jot that down and add it to the board. As she noted that she heard Stuart say, 'I don't think Wanda and Helga liked each other much.'

Sandy asked him why and he went on to tell his side of the story.

'I've only been looking after Wanda for the last six weeks, and she is hard work, but she really wanted this film and she was so happy when she got the part, but since she heard that Helga was playing her mother she seemed to change. It was strange, I heard her tell someone on the phone after Helga was murdered that she was glad, that's not right!' he whispered.

It was quiet for a while until Andy asked him another question, 'Do you know why she didn't like her?'

'Nope.' Stuart answered, 'I've no idea.'

Abi piped up, 'I think I do!'

Everyone looked at her and waited for her to say something else.

'And?' Andy urged.

'Well, I think Helga has met Wanda before, I think there's some history there and I think Helga knew something about Wanda that Wanda didn't want her to know.'

'What makes you think that?' Sandy asked.

Abi told everyone a tale about after Helga had finished her fitting on Sunday. Helga thought Abi had left the tent but she was in the back room with costumes when Wanda came in. They seemed to be arguing and although she couldn't hear everything, she did hear, something Helga said to Wanda. It was something like 'your just a little fraud'.

'I'm not sure what she meant. I tried to listen but all I heard was Wanda say 'I might be a fraud but you're a blackmailer'!

The whole table took an intake of breath.

'Did you tell the police that, when you were interviewed?' Sandy asked.

'No. I wasn't sure what was exactly said or what it was about, so I decided not to say anything. Plus they didn't really ask me the right question. They just asked where I was and things like that.'

Andy then said, 'Well here's dinner,' and the waitress started to hand out the meals.

Sandy thought that this was perfect timing and wished she could have had a note book to write this all down, but had to be satisfied that between her and Andy they would remember it all. Now the food had arrived the conversation changed to chitchat and Helga's murder was no longer the topic of conversation.

The food was fabulous and the evening was great, everyone got to know each other and new friendships where formed.

They left about eleven o'clock and they all gave each other the 'lovies' imaginary kiss on both cheeks. Once they got to the car, Andy let rip!

'Oh. My. Goodness!' he screeched, 'I think we have another suspect! Wanda, you sly thing. I wonder what Helga had on her, ooh! This is getting exciting! Let's get back to the murder room and write it all up! Home James!' he announced.

'Lucky his name is James.' Andy giggled. 'I've always wanted to say that!' Andy laughed to himself.

As soon as they got back they went into the 'Murder Room'. The boards were a bit bare now as they had removed Nancy and Guy's pictures from them. All that was left was the picture of Helga.

'So!' said Sandy. 'Let's get going.'

They found a picture of Wanda on the Internet, printed it out an added the picture to the board and wrote down as much as they could remember of the conversation Abi had overheard.

'I've got an idea!' said Sandy, 'It's a bit complicated, but I know how we can find out what was happening between the two of them.'

'Oh! Good, come on then, tell me?' Andy said.

Sandy sat down and explained the whole thing to Andy, he was going to have to play a part and Sandy was going to have to be rather clever so he wouldn't be recognised.

They sat for a while and worked it all out. It's a great plan and one where Andy's acting skills would be put to the test. They would have to clock in, in the morning on set to find out what jobs they have been assigned to, but that wouldn't stop them putting their plan into action. Andy looked pleased to be given such a great part to play.

It was late and time for Andy to go home and tomorrow they could set it all in action. As Andy left and said, 'I'll see you in the morning, bright and early.'

Sandy stood back and looked at the boards, thought about her plan and started to plotting in her head, how was she going to be creative. This was exciting, it was time for Sandy to really utilise her skills.

'To tomorrow!' She said out loud, left the room and closed the door.

Chapter 7

At seven o'clock the next morning Sandy was sitting in her car waiting for Andy to arrive on set. Suddenly there was a tap on the driver's window and a startled Sandy looked up from her notebook to see Andy waving profusely. Sandy smiled and got out of the car. Before she said anything Andy gushed, 'Ok! So I've started our plan and emailed Tamara Twist, Wanda's manager and asked if I can do an interview with Wanda. I said I was from the St Maarten Herald and that we want to do a special edition all about her. I'm sure I'll hear something back soon,' he gushed all in one breath.

'Brilliant!' Sandy said, 'Let's get going, so we can check in.'

They both walked off towards the portable cabin that was designated as 'The Office'. As they got there one of the assistant directors came out with some papers in his hand, as he saw them he said, 'Ah! Hi you two, you are just who I'm looking for. We've decided to cast another actor in Helga's role. She has agreed and we will fly her out by the end of the week. We have rearranged some of the shooting days and you both will be taking up the same job with the new actor. So, you're free to do whatever you want until she arrives. Enjoy the Island and have fun!' he added and turned round and went straight back into the office.

Sandy and Andy turned towards each other and high fived high in the air.

'Perfect!' Andy said, 'Now we can concentrate on catching a killer.'

Exactly at the same time he said that the door of the office opened again and out walked Lucas, the Chief of Police.

'Catching a killer, is all I heard. I hope you're not getting yourselves into trouble. You are only suppose to be my inside guys so you can find out any gossip,' he said. 'Be careful and don't do anything silly!' he added as he walked away to his car. Sandy could see him calling someone on his mobile, it was a short conversation, then he turned the engine on and left making his way back up the hill to the main road. Andy waited until he was well out of the way before he spoke again.

'Wow! That was close.' he said as his phone started ringing. Andy looked at the phone and then at Sandra who was lost in thought. He tried signaling, but Sandy wasn't watching but looking in her bag for something.

'Got it.' Sandy suddenly said and looked up. Andy was on the phone listening to someone talking to him. He carried on listening and then agreed to something. He said thank you and cut off the call and said, 'I've done it!' He made a little kick to celebrate. 'I've got an interview with Wanda. This afternoon at four o'clock. I've just got to arrange a place and let them know.'

'Well done,' said Sandy, 'Now, we need to create a character for you that she will not recognise, this is the fun bit. Any ideas on who you could be?' Sandy asked.

'Mmnnn...' Andy replied, 'I've been thinking about that and I think I should be like an American news reader, maybe a false nose and perfect hair, what do you think?' Andy asked.

Sandy thought for a minute and said, 'I think you should leave it to me. Where are you going to interview her?' she added.

'I think I should offer to interview her in her trailer, then she will feel happy and relaxed and she may talk to me. I'm going to bring champagne to loosen up the tongue and then, we can begin!' Andy said like he was the baddy in a pantomime.

Sandy thought that it was a good idea and they decided that before the meeting they would create some questions to put to Wanda. They took a drive to a coffee and pastry store to sit and work out a list. It didn't take long before they both became creative and put a list together.

1: Did you ever dream your life would be like it is?

2: Who do you look up to?

3: If you could play any part, what would it be?

And so on till they had about twenty questions.

Andy realised the main job was to get Wanda to open up, become his new best friend and tell him why she didn't like Helga and wanted her dead. Most of all he needed to work out if she was capable of murder, if she had a motive and if she was guilty, how did she do it? That was an awful lot to find out, but Andy was up for the challenge.

In fact he was excited to take on another character and put this plan into action.

At about one o'clock that afternoon they were back on the set and as Helga's trailer had been authorised for release by the police, they decided to use it for Andy's transformation. Sandy started to place everything she needed neatly out on the shelf. She chose a moustache and false nose, made out of prosthetics. A job like this was not easy and only a skilled makeup artiste would be capable of doing it. For Sandy it was a perfect challenge and she loved every minute of it. In today's world of High Definition it was only an expert who could carry off this type of transformation without making Andy look like a drag queen and stand up to scrutiny.

It took over two and a half hours to change Andy from Essex into Tim Crane from New York.

Andy didn't look during the whole transformation, in fact most of the time Sandy worked without a mirror until the last few minutes. Andy was swung round so he could see himself.

He was astounded! He looked so different that Wanda was not going to recognise him. He stood up and picked up a clipboard and started to talk with a New York accent.

'Hi Wanda, how are you? I'm so looking forward to chatting with you today, I've been a fan of your for ages, so let's sit, gossip and you can let me know why you killed Helga and how you did it OK?'

Sandy laughed out loud as he strolled up and down with a slight limp.

'How am I doing? Am I ready to go catch a murderer?' Andy asked.

'You look great, but forget the limp. That's a bit over the top.' Sandy said.

Just before four o'clock Sandy opened the trailer door and peeped outside to see who was around. She didn't want anyone to see the reporter leaving the trailer. She looked either side and motioned to Andy that it was all clear. Andy with his clipboard now full of paper and a pen stepped out and made his way towards Wanda's trailer. On his way he saw a guy doing some electrical work on a lighting rig. He looked familiar and Andy thought it was strange to see him on the set as he looked like the waiter who served them at 'Bamboo Bernies' when he and Helga first got to the Island. He shook his head and ignored it and carried on with the task ahead.

He knocked on the door and waited for a reply. Nothing happened, so he waited a couple more minutes and knocked again. This time the door opened. He couldn't see anyone behind then door. He looked in just as Wanda said, 'Come in! I'm just in the loo!'

Wanda Shore was primarily a recording artiste. She was originally from a small village in Sussex, England. She started her career just singing covers on YouTube until Universal Music spotted her and her career spun out of control. She has now become a superstar worldwide and she is pinning her whole career on this film. She's known as a bit of a madam in the business and Andy wasn't surprised at the greeting he had received. He popped his head in further and walked up the steps. He heard the chain pull and waited for Wanda to come out.

Andy hadn't met Wanda personally but he had been in a rehearsal room with her when he was with Helga in England. They had done a day rehearsing the upcoming scenes on the film before they flew out, but he sat at the back of the room as they rehearsed. He took a breath hoping he wouldn't be uncovered and smiled as the bathroom door opened and out stepped a very natural English beauty. She was about five foot five inches tall and very slim. She had very long jet black hair and bright blue stunning eyes. She was wearing a pair of torn jeans and a white t-shirt. She looked just like any young stylish lady and that made Andy feel a little bit more at ease.

He started off the conversation with, 'Hi, My name is Tim Crane and I'm from the St Maarten Herald.' he said with a New York accent, 'By the way I've bought you a great bottle of champagne and…' He was interrupted by Wanda as she said, 'Brilliant, I could so do with this, I hope you're going to join me.'

Andy couldn't believe how easy it was to get her to open the bottle.

'Of course.' He answered.

Wanda opened the bottle like an expert and poured two classes. Her trailer was even bigger than Helga's, it was a phenomenal. It had everything you could want, a sitting room, kitchen, makeup and hair room and two bedrooms. He knew, as he had to walk through some of it following Wanda. She wanted to do this interview from the small room at one end of the trailer that looked rather like an office. It had a desk, plus a sofa and two chairs. She sat on the sofa and motioned for Andy (Tim) to sit on one of the chairs. She was wearing a flowing kaftan with a bikini underneath, her long hair was perfect and she had dark glasses on. Andy wasn't sure why she needed them on inside, but never mind.

'She started the conversation with, 'I love St Maarten its so sunny and beautiful, I'm hooked!'

Andy made a small giggle and asked if it was Ok to record the interview on his mobile phone. Wanda agreed and poured herself another glass as the first one had gone. She seemed to be talking rather fast, so maybe she didn't like interviews.

He wanted to make her feel comfortable, so he started chatting about what it was like to be 'Wanda.' She was very open and talked about how she had lost her freedom and although that was the price of fame, she sometimes felt lonely.

Andy was shocked that Wanda was prepared to chat that openly, but carried on asking questions.

He choose to talk to her as if they where friends just sitting down having a gossip. Andy was very aware that in fifteen minutes she had drunk four glasses of Champagne and the more she drank the more she answered his questions with gusto!

He decided to get to the nitty gritty and asked, 'How did you feel when you found out that Helga Beaumont had been killed.'

The mood changed drastically and Wanda removed her glasses. Andy expected her to either pretend to cry with fake tears that she was sorry, or get annoyed that she had been asked that question. Neither happened. Instead she said, 'If you think I should be sorry that bitch is dead, you must be joking!' And she downed the whole glass of champagne and immediately poured another one, that last one in the bottle and then said, 'Fuck it, it's all gone!'

Andy didn't move an eyelash, he just said he knew where another bottle was and he could get back in five minutes with it. By now Wanda wasn't 100% with it and just nodded. Andy got up to leave and told her he would be back quickly. He left and immediately ran into the other trailer where

Sandy was camped. She was surprised to see him so quickly as he just said, 'I'm not stopping, I need another bottle of something, what have we got.' Andy started rummaging through the kitchen.

'They must have left stuff for Helga,' he said frantically.

Andy opened the fridge and found a bottle of white wine.

'Bingo!' he shouted, picked it up spun round and told Sandy he was off again.

He ran back into the other trailer and showed Wanda the bottle. Her reaction was, 'I don't think I should drink anymore, it makes me say things I shouldn't.'

Andy then said to her, 'I have an idea! lets go off the record, here. I'll turn the phone off and we can just chat.'

Wanda looked at him suspiciously as Andy said, 'Didn't you like Helga then?'

'What that bitch!' Wanda spouted.

'For some reason she hated me, I've no idea why, I only met her for the first time in London at a rehearsal the director had, so all the actors could meet each other. I've no idea why the bitch hated me so much, but it was obvious from the start. The only thing I could think of was that she was about to play my mother and I don't think she liked that. I don't think she like going from being a lead character in a soap opera to a supporting actor in a film. She thought she was better than supporting pop star. That's my view anyway. So I'm glad someone finished her off!'

Andy remained impassive and just listened.

'I don't know who she thought she was, just some old 'has been' from 'The Helter Skelter' and that's finished just like she is.' Wanda laughed and put her glasses back on.

'I wish I had come up with the idea of finishing her off, but unfortunately I didn't. Someone got there before I did, but here is a toast to them. To the killing of a blackmailer!' she raised her glass and downed the drink in one go.

At that moment a big stocky man walked into the room of the trailer and said, 'Ok, enough! That's all for now folks. Time for you to pack up and leave the trailer.'

Andy realised the man meant business, he had no idea who he was, but he needed to be obeyed.

He wanted to ask what she meant by calling Helga a blackmailer, but he knew his time was up. Andy thanked Wanda and said, 'I'm so pleased we could chat, thank you for the interview.' and left, leaving the man to help Wanda into another room.

Andy made his way back to the other trailer where Sandy was waiting. As soon as he stepped in Sandy wanted to know every detail. Andy told her that he had taped the whole thing including the bit that he said was off the record. He hadn't turned it off. So they sat and listened to the whole interview again.

When it finished Sandy told him that he had done a brilliant job and what did he think about her confession. Andy said he thought that she didn't have anything to do with the murder but there was more to the story than they knew. Why did Helga dislike Wanda so much and what was the toast about blackmailing? If in fact Helga was blackmailing Wanda, why did someone get rid of her to stop it?

'Maybe it was that big bully that walked in and stop the interview.' Andy suggested.

Sandy agreed and said, 'What happened at the end?'

'I just left,' he said.

They sat and chatted about the whole interview and Sandy said she wanted to know who this guy was.

'Just call Lucas, he will know.' Suggested Andy.

Sandy thought it was a great idea and at the same time she could let him know a little bit about the interview, just to keep him happy. So Sandy called Lucas and asked who the big guy was that hangs around with Wanda. He explained that it was Brian Jones, Wanda's manager. Sandy went on to tell him that they had managed to chat away with Wanda without her knowing what was going on and they had found out that Wanda and Helga didn't like each other much, but they working on finding out more. Lucas appreciated her help and said, 'Keep going, you are in a valuable position inside the production team to chat and not be suspicious, it's a real help, thank you.' The call ended.

Sandy told Andy who the guy was and they decided to go back to Sandy's and do some research on actually who Brian Jones is and his background.

When they got back Sandy worked on her laptop and Andy on his iPad, it didn't take long before they found out all about Brian and what he looked like. He was about five feet ten inches tall and a big build. He looked like he could be a builder with big muscles and lots of tattoos.

WIKIPEDIA: Brian Jones, Age 36.

Brian began in the music business at the age of fifteen selling CD's of his friends. He took on his first management role, looking after the management of his friend D Freemont the wrapper. D Freemont went on to become a Platinum selling recording artiste. He then spent three years in prison for fraud after embezzling two million pounds of D Freemont's money. After getting out of prison D Freemont went back to the music business and up to date he works as Manager to Wanda Shore.

Andy spouted, 'I knew he was dodgy, he looked like a thug. So maybe he knows why Helga was blackmailing Wanda and maybe he 'did her in'. He looks that type. But how the hell are we going to get him to talk?'

'Who was the guy that is Wanda's security, we met him at dinner? Sandy asked.

'That was Tom.' Andy answered. 'Why, what do you think he can do?'

Sandy explained that maybe he wasn't part of it, if they got him on side and explained what they knew then he might help them.

Andy was dubious and asked, 'How do we know for definite that he wasn't involved?'

'I think we need Lucas to help us with that task, if we ask him to check for us, we can move forward.'

'Ok try it,' said Andy.

Sandy called Lucas and asked how much he knows about Tom, Wanda's security. Lucas laughed and said, 'He is completely innocent. He is a British detective; seconded here for the term of the film, if you need his help, just ask. Tell him I told you. He was asked to be with Wanda as she has a stalker in the UK and he is here to protect her. They think the stalker may follow her here.'

Sandy asked one question, 'Does Brian know who he really is?'

'No.' Lucas answered. 'Tom decided that only Wanda and I should know.'

Sandy thanked him and put the phone down. Andy heard it all as she had it on loudspeaker.

Andy said, 'This is getting very complicated, but getting Tom involved sounds great, it gives us an insider and we can tell him what we know. I'm sure he will help. He is a nice guy.'

Andy once again looked at his crew sheet and got Tom's number and called him. He told him that they were working with Lucas and the St Maarten police and that they have some information that he may like to hear about, as he might be able to help them. Tom said that Wanda was asleep so he could pop over. Andy gave him the address and he told them he would be about fifteen minutes. He was exactly right. Fifteen minutes later there was a knock on the door. Tom had arrived.

Tom came in and listened to the recording of the interview. As it finished he looked confused.

'Ok. So, I thought you had some info about Wanda's stalker. This is totally different. If Wanda was being blackmailed by Helga, then what did Helga know and that makes me think, did Brian have something to do with Helga's death.'

'Precisely,' said Sandy and Andy at the same time. 'That's what we thought,' finished Sandy.

They sat at the table had chatted about the situation. Tom explained that Wanda was good at sharing info with him. 'She trusts me,' he said, 'I think the best thing I can do is be honest, I'm going to tell Wanda we suspect that Brian has something to do with Helga's death. Then I can ask her what did Helga have over her.'

They both agreed that Tom knew best, and as this murder was the first time Sandy and Andy had ever been involved in one, they had to trust him.

'When will you ask her?' said Sandy.

'As soon as I can,' he replied, 'I need to wait until Brian isn't around and then I'll give it a go. So, one question, how come you two are digging around a murder?'

'Well, we kind of fell into it,' said Andy.

'It's more like we are hidden on the inside and Lucas, The Chief of Police here in St Maarten, asked us for help. We are little enough to stay hidden and annoying enough to ask lots of questions without people being suspicious.' Sandy explained.

'Ok, That explains it.' Tom answered.

'I've got an idea!' Sandy said. From the conversation we can surmise that Wanda is rather lonely, so let's invite her here for dinner It will be just the four of us, that way we can all chat together,' she added.

'I can try.' Tom said. 'I'll chat to her when she wakes up, but it may not be easy to get her away from Brian. I'm supposed to be protecting her, but he seems to be everywhere. I'll speak to you later.' He left.

The two of them were silent for a while after Tom left. They both sat there thinking until Andy spoke. 'It's a bit scary, isn't it. I've just realised.' Andy murmured.

'What's scary?' Sandy asked.

'Tom just brought things to life. We are playing around with a murderer.' Andy uttered quietly.

'Were not playing with a murderer Andy, were just helping the police with their inquiries. We are not actually hanging around with one.' Sandy added.

Andy took a moment and changed his thoughts to food. 'I'm starving, let's get something to eat,' he shouted, 'It might take my mind off who did it.' Andy made his way into Sandy's kitchen and opened the fridge.

'Help yourself!' Sandy shouted, and he did!

Chapter 8

It wasn't until the next morning that they heard from Tom to say they were all set for dinner at seven o'clock that evening. He explained that Wanda was excited and thanked them very much for the invitation. Andy went over to Sandy's in the morning and they chatted as they got organised for dinner.

Sandy suggested a barbeque and Andy wanted to create a Michelin Star creation. Sandy stopped Andy as he was describing a mouth watering, very complicated dish,

'Andy,' she said. He completely ignored her and went on to create an imaginary mouth watering dessert.

'Andy!' Sandy said again, but this time a little louder, but there was still no stopping him as he had gone into a complete trance of culinary delight. This time Sandy shouted at Andy and clipped him around the ear, 'We are having a barbeque.' She announced and Andy nodded, realising this was not the time to argue. They decided to spend the day finding out all about Helga and her background, which may help to explain why she was killed.

Sandy told Andy all she knew, which wasn't very much. Although Sandy had seen Helga nearly every day for many years, they only spoke about really mundane things. Helga would spend most of her time either asleep or gossiping. The only other conversation would be about her husbands, children and colleague's. Sandy then remembered that Helga was having problems with her daughter. She was a spoilt brat who now would be about twenty-four years old.

'If I remember,' Sandy said, 'Tamara is her name. The last conversation I remember having about her was something about a bad crowd she got in with. She wasn't working and Helga was getting fed up.' Sandy went on to explain everything she could remember about Tamara.

Tamara had gone to a top class private school from the age of four, with Helga working such long hours she wasn't really part of her childhood. Between nannies and school there wasn't much time for Tamara to bond with her mother. In fact

Helga often felt like Tamara was an annoyance, she really wasn't a natural mother and even giving Tamara a bath or reading to her at night was rare. In fact Tamara was only two when Helga went into rehab, so her nanny was more like a mother than a nanny. Tamara had a great nanny from the time she was born until she was four years old and started school. Her nanny then became ill and passed away shortly after. This devastated the young Tamara and she never really bonded with another nanny, but went through them like blocks of cheese. By the time she was thirteen she was a promiscuous and stroppy teenager. Helga was not in control and this was a big part of why her three marriages didn't work. Tamara was in control and ruled the roost. Helga just wanted an easy life. She was selfish and now her daughter was not only selfish too, but stubborn and emotionally lost. Since she left school at eighteen she travelled and went from one job to another, never staying anywhere more than a month. Helga was always bailing her out of one problem or another. All Tamara wanted was her money and to move on to the next adventure. All Helga wanted was peace.

Then about two years ago, Tamara got in with a bad crowd. She started taking drugs and partying too hard. The last conversation Helga had with Sandy about Tamara was to say that she had had enough of her lying and stealing. She was at the end of her tether.

'Wow!' said Andy, 'that sounds like a motive to murder. Money. Maybe Helga had threatened to cut her off!'

Sandy said nothing but just looked at Andy strangely, 'But to murder your mother, surely not? I remember her when she was just four years old and her nanny had just died, she was such a sweet thing, Helga would bring her into work and she would help me clean the brushes and I would do her makeup, but murder? No! I can't believe that. Plus she isn't here. She couldn't have murdered her. She isn't even on the island. That also makes me think. I wonder if she will be flying out here, or if they've even found her and told her. They must have done, it's been all over the media. I haven't even turned on the television to watch it. Sorry.' Sandy said realising that she had been babbling.

'Maybe she got someone to do it for her?' Andy suggested.

'Ok, we can't rule it out, but lets look and see if there is anyone else,' Sandy said.

'What about her husband's?' Andy asked.

I never met the first one, Tamara's dad. He was a bit of a crook. If I remember he went to prison just before Helga got the job on 'The Helter Skelter', it was fraud. I can't remember exactly what he did but it was something to do with dodgy mortgages. The second one was a real charmer. He used to come to the set with Helga and was forever pinching bums and trying to get a sneaky kiss from any of the girls. He was a total womaniser and eventually she had enough. That only lasted about two years. The last one lasted even less time. I knew she shouldn't of married him, but I couldn't have said anything, as it wasn't my place to. She was only married about four months. It was during this time that Tamara totally went off the rails.

'His name was Clint. That should have given it away. He batted for the other side and just wanted a marriage as a front. He was an actor too in 'Too far to go' the rival soap on 'The other side'. She caught him in bed with his co-star and that was that. She vowed she would never marry again. So that is all of Helga's husbands.'

'Doesn't sound like any of them would want to kill her?' Andy said. 'I do have a question though, have the police checked her phone calls and bank accounts just to see if anything strange happened just before she was killed? Just so we can rule out stuff,' Andy asked.

'Well done Andy,' said Sandy, 'Great question, I'll call Lucas and ask.'

Sandy called Lucas and got no joy as Lucas said they had checked both and no unusual calls or payments had gone in or out.

'Ok!' said Andy. 'What's our next plan of action?'

They decided to go to the supermarket to buy the food for their special dinner with Wanda. They got in the car and Sandy asked Andy where was the best place to shop. She had only been to the local supermarket when she got there to stock up on basics. Andy suggested the Simply Supermarket over on the French side. So off they went and drove through Cupecoy, which had the most incredible views over to the French side of the Island. They made their way to the supermarket chatting about anything and everything on the way.

Suddenly as they were driving over the hill, a motorbike sped passed them. They kept going up the hill and just as they got to the top the man on the motor bike was standing there with his bike on its side, make signals at them to stop.

Sandy started to pull over, as Andy said, 'Be careful Sandy, this could be one of their tricks, I've heard all about it!' At that point the man came over to the car shouting loudly and banging on the passenger window accusing Sandy of driving into his bike.

'I haven't hit anything, I would know about it!' she shouted back at the local.

'You're a bloody liar!' Andy shouted whilst staying in the safety of the car.

Sandy went to get out and Andy pulled her back saying, 'Tell him you're going to call the police, that will stop him!'

Sandy shouted, 'Give me my bag then, get my phone!' Andy shuffled through Sandy's bag, got out the phone and shook it at the window, then passed it over. They both shouted in unison, 'We are going to call the police!' Sandy pretending to dial the number as the man huffed and left shouting a pile of abuse as he got on his motor bike and drove off. Both Sandy and Andy sat back and sighed. Andy broke the silence with, 'Wow! That was close!'

'Cheeky bugger!' Sandy added. 'I can't believe the cheek of it, as if we would fall for a cheap trick like that!'

'Plenty of people do.' Andy added. 'I've seen all about it on a forum. There are lots of people throughout the world that chat about the Island, I was doing some research before I came out and I came across this forum where they were talking about crime on the island. Someone had posted this story exactly how it just happened. It was only because they did the police phone call trick, that I knew what to do,' he continued.

'Thank goodness you did, I'm not sure I would have thought of it that quickly. Ok Let's get going, how far from here is the supermarket?' Sandy asked.

Andy explained that it was only about a mile down the road.

Sandy drove off and carried on muttering about the cheek of the guy on the bike. Andy kept quiet and just showed Sandy where the supermarket was. Sandy parked up and was just about to get out of the car when she had a light bulb moment.

'Oh no!' she uttered, pulling Andy back roughly into the car by his t-shirt.

'What?' Andy spluttered sitting back in the passenger seat.

'Who is going to meet Wanda, Andy or Tim Crane?' Sandy said worryingly.

Andy sat back and thought. She can't meet Tim, as Tom doesn't know anything about Tim. Bloody hell. Tim, Tom, Andy, Sandy. It's all getting a bit confusing.

'OK! So I wonder what Tom has said about who we are and why we would want to invite them over for dinner?' Andy added thoughtfully.

'Maybe he just said, some of the crew have invited them or...I don't know, why don't I just ask him.' Sandy said.

'Good idea!' agreed Andy.

Sandy called Tom and asked him exactly what he had said to Wanda, just so they have the story straight. He told her that he wanted to introduce her to some friends of his and that's all he said. Sandy relayed that to Andy as they made their way into the supermarket.

Sandy and Andy walked up and down each aisle putting all they needed into the dodgy small trolley that had a mind of its own. Chicken, steak and lots of French bread and salad was added.

'Ok!' Sandy announced, 'What's for dessert?' They moved along to the fresh cake counter and chose amazing gateaux.

'I think we have everything we need.' Sandy said as they made their way to the check out desk. Sandy was just putting the shopping on the cash desk as her phone rang. She asked Andy to take over as she answered it.

Chapter 9

'Hello! Is dat Sandy?' a deep Caribbean voice sung, 'Dis is Alan your friendly driver!'

'Hello Alan.' Sandy replied.

'Now,' Alan went on to say, 'I've got dis amazing opportunity if you're interested. Someone has cancelled a two-hour boat trip and de boats just sitting here. Do ya fancy joining us? And dat Andy, can he come too?' Alan added as an afterthought.

Andy was just paying for the barbeque food as Sandy walked towards him. She put her hand over the phone and told him what Alan had said. Andy jumped up and down a couple of times and nodded profusely. Then he asked, 'Were is the boat?'

Sandy asked Alan and relayed back, that it was at the lagoon moored up at Skipjacks. Andy knew exactly where that was and they both agreed to go. They had plenty of time as it was just coming up to midday. They could do the boat trip and get back and prepare dinner in plenty of time. They also decided between them that they deserved a trip as all they had done for days was investigate and now it was going to be a couple of hours to relax.

'What about all this food?' Andy said, we couldn't leave it in this heat. Sandy thought for a while and then darted over to the barbeque section and picked up a cold box.

'This will do the trick,' she told Andy and then added, 'We can always use one, so perfect.'

Andy paid for the cold box and they packed up the food, packed the car and made their way back around the island to Skipjacks. The roads were quite clear and they made it in about twenty minutes.

As they walked through Skipjacks Restaurant, Sandy could see the blue waters of the lagoon at the end. Although they had driven around the lagoon, she hadn't taken much notice of it before. As they came up towards the boat named 'Random Winds' Sandy thought to herself that this wasn't the kind of boat she expected. She expected a motor powered boat, where she would just sit and relax. This was a beautiful boat but it had sails! Andy tapped Sandy on the shoulder gently and whispered, 'It's got sails! Does that mean we have to do something?'

'I really hope not!' answered Sandy and carried on walking towards the boat. They saw Alan chatting to someone and as he saw them he turned round and the other person disappeared onto the boat.

'Hi guys!' he announced, 'Glad you could make it, let's go on board and have sum fun!' he said in his Caribbean drawl.

They followed Alan onto the boat as he put out his hand to steady the task.

Once on board they were introduced to Saul, the captain. He was a tanned Italian who was wearing a vest like top, very short shorts and had a deep tan as if he spent most of his life in the sun. He was a jolly fellow, but Sandy wasn't sure if that was his nature or if he had already been on the island rum. They were shown to the seats at the back of the boat and Alan offered them a drink. They both decided on a fruit punch so they could keep their wits about them. Andy started to look petrified, and whispered to Sandy, 'I don't really like boats!'

Sandy turned round and laughed. 'It's a bit late to tell me now, we are just about to leave. Are you ok? Why did you agree to come then?' Sandy asked all in one breath.

Andy looked a bit green but took a deep breath and explained, 'I've always been afraid of the water. I'm not a good swimmer in fact I think swimming is just for saving lives not for pleasure, but I thought this may help me get over my worries. I didn't expect to be this scared!'

Sandy tried to placate him and told him he would be fine.

'They use this boat for trips every day of the year. I'm sure it's very safe.'

Andy just nodded and hoped for the best. But looked petrified.

Sandy looked out over the lagoon. It was a perfect setting, blue waters and mega yachts owned by the rich and famous. She could smell the flowers and greenery that nestled on the water's edge. She could see the fish swimming through the clear Caribbean waters. She closed her eyes and wished she could remember this moment forever. Suddenly the boat moved as it left the dock and Andy could be seen eyes wide as he clung onto the side of the boat. Alan came up from the galley and gave them their two fruit cocktails. He told them that Corin was below deck making some lunch, which would be served very soon. Andy didn't look like he wanted anything to eat ever again, but Sandy was hungry and looked forward to whatever was being served up.

They made their way out of the lagoon, as the Simpson Bay Bridge lifted, and out to the Caribbean Sea. It was a clear sunny day with a slight wind. Sandy had never been on a sailboat and relished the opportunity to just relax and watch everything go past. Andy wasn't quite so relaxed, he still looked a little green, but he sipped on his fruit punch and tried hard to relax. As least his hold on the side of the boat had relaxed slightly.

A Caribbean gentleman with two large platters emerged from the galley. He laid the two platters on the table in front of them and disappeared again into the depths of the boat. The platters were laden with a large selection of fruits and fish and salad, beautifully prepared and placed with great care. Alan then emerged with plates and cutlery and all three of them sat down and started to eat.

'This is so kind of you.' Sandy said to Alan.

'Dis is no problem!' he replied, 'Silly letting da food and trip go to waste, we was all ready to go and de family called me and cancelled. Dey had already paid de bill! So no worries...be happy!'

Sandy smiled to herself as she heard the sound of Bob Marley being played from the galley. Sun, great food, the Caribbean Sea and a cocktail. How did life get this good? She closed her eyes and mentally remembered this moment as if her memory was a photo album to be brought out and looked over occasionally.

Suddenly the peace was forgotten as Sandy thought she heard someone shout PIRATES on the starboard! She opened her eyes with a start and although she was bewildered, she saw all three of the crew start to run around.

Her first thought was to think she was dreaming, but soon realised she was wide-awake and about to be part of a nightmare. She looked over to Andy who was paralyzed with fear and looking straight ahead as if to say 'if I move my head, this could be real'. Then he muttered, 'Pirates? Here? Now and after us?'

Without a chance to answer, Sandy saw Alan coming towards them with haste and he said, 'I'm sorry guys, you will need to go inside, der has been spate of modern day pirates, trying to steal boats. It looks like dey are after us.'

'Us.' Andy mouthed. 'After us!' he repeated, 'Now!' he added in a panic. Andy looked over to where a large boat was coming fast towards the horizon. He could see in the distance that a powerboat was coming towards them. Inside it looked like there were about four men who were waving guns, bloody large guns.

Up until now Sandy hadn't said anything but just got up to move inside to safety. She glanced over to the boat coming towards them at a great speed and paused for a spit second.

Her brain went into survival mode. Pirates? In the Caribbean? A bit cliché if you ask me, she thought to herself. Then she took a last look before disappearing into the galley of the boat, just behind Andy. Alan stayed up on deck and Sandy just caught the look on his face as the chef also ran passed her and followed Alan to the deck above. Alan had a smirk on his face. Sandy started to get suspicious and whispered to Andy, but he was curled up in the fetal position on a little cushioned seat under a porthole.

'Andy!' she whispered, 'I think we are the recipients of a joke and the joke is on us!'

Andy looked up sheepishly and said, 'A Joke? There aren't any pirates?'

Sandy nodded and put her finger first to her lips and then motioned Andy to be quiet and follow her. They both made their way to the tiny toilet on board and huddled inside together. There wasn't much room and they shifted around repeatedly so that they could close the door! Sandy whispered to Andy, 'If we stay in here, when the so-called pirates come aboard, they will think they have lost us, or that we have jumped overboard. Maybe we can swap the joke round on them.'

'My leg has gone numb already.' Andy said in pain. 'I'm not sure I will last that long without passing out.'

'I don't think we will be here long. Shhhhhh, something's happening.' They both went quiet.

They could hear faint talking outside the room.

'Where have they gone?' a voice said.

'I left them both here only minutes ago.' someone else answered.

'Maybe they have fallen overboard.' the first voice said.

Sandy put her hand across Andy's mouth to stop him laughing.

'Well you better find them Alan, before we get accused of murder. One murder on set is enough for any film.'

Sandy wanted to jump out and say 'the jokes on you', but decided they deserved just a little longer to worry. Sandy and Andy heard footsteps and then quiet. So Sandy took the opportunity to open the toilet door very slightly. They both popped their heads out and couldn't see anyone. Sandy crept out with Andy following just behind. Sandy walked through the galley and picked up a huge meat cleaver and a carving knife. She gave the knife to Andy and kept the eat cleaver for herself. She motioned for them both to hold it high. They crept up the galley steps and onto the deck with Sandy in the lead.

'Talk about women and children first! Where does that leave you?' Sandy said to Andy very, very quietly.

Sandy could just see the three crew members of the Random Winds and three others, all in pirate costumes arguing. She motioned to Andy and whispered to him. With knives held high, both of them ran up the stairs and towards the pirates screaming, 'Arrrr, me hearty.' In deep throaty voices.

All six of the men just stood there petrified whilst a woman and a flamboyant man flew towards them with knives held high and screaming.

Panic ensued. The Italian skipper dived off the side with the cook not far behind. The three 'pirates' huddled together and put their heads down, whilst Alan just stood there with his glowing white smile and an amused smirk on his face and a drink in his hand. Still singing 'Don't worry be happy!'

Sandy and Andy stopped and fell into hysterics. Sandy started to cry with laughter as Andy tried hard not to wet himself. All three of the pirates put their hands in the air and simultaneously shouted, 'We give up!'

Sandy put her cleaver down and took the knife off of Andy, as he looked dangerous uncontrollably laughing with a knife in his hand. The first pirate looked up and said, 'Sorry! We were only following orders!'

All three of them looked familiar but Sandy wasn't sure where she knew them from. They admitted very quickly that they were stunt men on the film set and that Mark Fleece, Guy Drovane's PA, had asked them to do it. One of the guys came forward and said, 'I think Mark was pissed because he has to be on set every day and Andy's got himself a holiday. So as we were filming today he asked us to stay in costume and play along. Somehow Mark got Alan in on the joke too. Sorry Andy, it was suppose to be a bit of fun!'

'Fun!' Andy shouted. My employer has been murdered and Mark thinks I'm shirking work. Wait until I get hold of him, he might be the next murder victim!'

With that, Saul the captain peaked over the side of the boat and said, 'Is it safe to come back on board?' shortly followed by a very wet cook who tried to get back on board but slipped off a couple of times before someone went over the help him up. He muttered all the way to the steps and went back into the safety of the galley.

Alan shouted, 'Drinks all?' and went and fetched a bottle of rum. They all had a rum cocktail and talked about how funny the little adventure had been.

'Please tell Mark,' Andy said, 'To be scared, be very scared! And that I WILL get my own back, but I am patient.'

They all laughed and the three wayward pirates got back onto their boat and sped off. A short while later, the rest of them started to make their way back into Simpson Bay. It was an uneventful journey back and thank goodness for that, they had had quite enough adventure for one day. They said goodbye to all on deck and made their way back to the car.

Sitting on the dock was the same man Sandy saw at the photo shop in Phillipsburg. He was drinking a beer and watching them. Sandy turned her back to him and said to Andy quietly, 'See that man over there?'

Andy turned, looked and said, not very quietly, 'Where?'

Sandy turned back around and the man was gone.

'It's ok,' she said. 'I think I'm just being foolish. Ignore me.'

Andy shrugged his shoulders as they got in the car.

Sandy had a good look around but the man was nowhere to be seen. She had a sinister feeling in her gut and her gut was never wrong.

It was now nearly four o'clock in the afternoon and time to go and get ready for dinner. They got back to the Condo, unloaded the car and they decided to split the jobs to prepare the dinner. It was very quiet in the Condo as they both got down to their individual tasks, when suddenly there was a loud knock on the door. They both looked at each other and Sandy nodded at Andy as if to say you go. Andy nodded back a definite NO! Another knock and this time it was even louder. Someone was angry! Sandy went to answer it and as she turned the handle, the door was pushed forward and it knocked Sandy across the room.

'How rude...' She started to say out loud, as Guy Drovane stormed in shouting.

Sandy had only seen Guy on the big screen and she had been a fan since she was a teenager. She had had a poster on her bedroom wall, but she never expected him to walk into her home, especially looking like he had steam coming out of his ears.

'How dare you!' he started, 'How dare you accuse my wife of being a murderer, who are you two? What the hell are you doing going around asking questions and delving into matters that are no concern of yours? You need to be deported. Sent back and hung drawn and quartered.'

'That's a bit extreme isn't it?' Andy stated.

'Only figuratively speaking not literally, you imbecile!'

'Look!' Sandy spluttered, 'We are helping the Chief of Police with the investigation and someone dropped of this package outside our door.'

She went into the 'Murder Room' and came out with the package, handed it over to Guy and watched him open it.

'So you see we had to talk to her, even if it was to ensure the police didn't investigate her. That would have been a lot worse.'

'But why you two?' He asked calming down a bit and sitting himself down on a sofa.

'Take a seat.' Andy said quietly and sarcastically.

Sandy carried on with, 'No one would expect us to be working for them, it means that we can go around asking questions. Where some people wouldn't want to talk to the police they would talk to us instead. We can be discreet. We haven't said anything about your hospital visit to anyone.'

Andy quietly butted in with, 'I might have told... only joking!'

Guy gave Andy a filthy look and turned back to Sandy.

'But who dropped the envelope off?' Guy asked.

'We think it was Nancy's driver, but to be honest as it wasn't important to the murder investigation, we haven't looked into it. We will leave that to you.'

By now Guy had calmed down a bit and Sandy offered him a drink. Guy accepted and Sandy went to pour a glass of local rum. Andy just sat there saying nothing. He wasn't happy at being called an imbecile and he was showing his anger in his body and face. Guy downed the drink in one go and started to talk.

'We met about sixteen years ago now. Helga was just starting off in her career. I fell in love with her, the first time I saw her. She was married and so was I. I wanted to see her, but my morals didn't let me. Then she got divorced from her first husband and we sort of fell into a relationship. I loved her, but could not face telling Nancy, so we drifted, in and out of a relationship for fifteen years. She would reconnect every time she got divorced or had a row with her latest beau. I think she knew I would never leave Nancy, but somehow fifteen years went past. I couldn't kill her. I wouldn't have hurt a hair on her head. I had to finish it for good. I told Nancy I had and I promised her it wouldn't start up again. That bit is true at least!'

Both Sandy and Andy sat there and listened. Andy had calmed down and a tear could be seen falling slowly down his cheek. He wiped it away and listened.

'I'll miss her." he announced, which broke the silence, 'And now it's time I went.' he said as he stood up.

'I hope you will carry on keeping my whereabouts at the time of the murder to yourselves, at least you know none of us where involved. So let me say good night and I'm sure I'll see you again. Probably on set.'

With that he left. Sandy and Andy stayed where they were and in silence. Sandy disturbed it by saying, 'Wow! That was intense!'

Andy stood up and announced rather dramatically, 'Come on Sandy we have a meal to create and a mission to attend to. They will be here soon and we are not ready, so all hands on deck and let's get going!'

'OOOh!' Sandy answered. 'Who made you boss? And less comments about decks please, after this afternoon I may not be venturing on board a boat for a while!'

They spent the next half an hour finishing the food. Just as they had that done there was a knock on the door. In walked Tom with Wanda behind him, she looked uncomfortable and a little shy. So different from the persona she adopted on stage or with the media. She was wearing a pair of denim shorts and a loose white blouse. Her long hair was twisted and place on the top of her head by one black clip. She looked relaxed and casual.

'Wanda these are my friends, this is Sandy and this is Andy. Please don't think they are normally this quiet, because I promise you they are not,' he added.

'Who me? I'm like a little mouse.' Andy told her and she smiled for the first time.

'Come and sit down on the patio.' Sandy offered, 'We are all very casual here. I'll pour the first drink, then its go for yourselves. Ok?'

Wanda nodded and sat down and seemed to take a big sigh.

'That's a big sigh.' Andy said.

'It's been a hard few weeks, this is a fabulous view.' Wanda said changing the conversation.

'Where are you staying?' Sandy asked her. Wanda looked at Tom as if to ask permission. Tom nodded and said 'It's Ok Wanda we are with friends, there is nothing you can't talk about here, I promise. It's like I said before we came. Sandy and Andy are the good guys, I promise you.'

'I'm sorry.' Wanda said. 'It's been a long time since I could be myself. I've gone from being a...a no one into this person who is suspicious of everyone and a hideaway. It's not the life I expected. I'm staying in a private Condo at Pelcan Key.'

Both Sandy and Andy sympathized and Andy told her enthusiastically, 'While you are here, you are just Wanda. Sit, drink and relax. Is Wanda your real name?'

Wanda hesitated and nodded.

Sandy wasn't so sure as she really seemed reticent to agree. Suspicious, she thought to herself and then shrugged it off as she instructed Andy to light the barbeque. Sandy went into the kitchen and came out with a pitcher of rum punch and they all drank and chatted. The mood was really light and they enjoyed the food and drink. They had kept on neutral subjects, so there wasn't any bad feeling.

Andy wasn't that patient and all of a sudden asked, 'Do you know who your new mum is going to be? On the film I mean.'

'No, I know they have asked someone though. They said they are waiting on an answer, anything is better than the last one!' she added with a whisper.

'You didn't get on with Helga then?' Sandy asked.

'No!' she answered through gritted teeth.

'Had you known her for long?' Andy added as he refilled her glass.

'It's a long story,' she said, 'And not a particularly nice one!' She added as she downed her drink, slowly, in one go, as if she wanted to tell but was unsure.

'It's ok.' Sandy said sympathetically, you're with friends. If you want to share, we are listening.' They all waited in anticipation.

With that Wanda spilled the beans...the whole tin!

Chapter 10

Wanda admitted that she came from a rather poor family where her dad had left when she was about three years old. Her mum brought Wanda and her three siblings up on her own with very little money. Wanda was the youngest and she was virtually bought up by her older brother and two sisters. Survival was the name of the game every day. Her mum, Sheila, went from one man to another and Wanda never had a good male role model. She didn't know any of her grandparents either, as her parents ran off at age seventeen together and got married against their parent's wishes. Both families disowned their kids. Wanda was bought up in Walthamstow in East London. An area where 80% of families were on state benefits. Hope wasn't in the young people's thinking, but just feeding their continuing hunger or how they would pay the bills. They thought nothing of packing up in minutes and escaping to a new house, as the bills couldn't be paid. Wanda didn't understand what was happening, but just abided by the families wants.

When Wanda was eleven and started at the local high school, she learnt how to toughen up. She had to, to survive. It was a big school and if she didn't want to be bullied she had to become the bully. A phase in her life she didn't feel good about. When she was about thirteen she saw a notice outside the main hall about a choir audition. Whilst standing staring at the poster a little voice said, 'Are you thinking of joining the choir?'

'No.' She answered defensively and rather rudely.

But the girl didn't take no for an answer. She told her that her name was Suzy and that she had been in the choir for over a year and she loved it and then went on to tell her that they go out and perform all around the country and even in theatres.

This made Wanda think and gruffly she told Suzy she would consider it. Her escape had always been music, any forms of music. So she decided to go for it and try and get into the choir.

The auditions were being held in the Drama department in the schools studio theatre. The poster had said that she had to prepare a song. She didn't know any, so she had borrowed her older brothers iPod, which he had probably stolen from some innocent bystander. She had no choice but to sing one of the songs on it. She was really limited by the amount of music she would have been able to sing, as most of the songs on the iPod were rap. But suddenly she came across a song called 'What's it gonna be' by an American band called En Vogue. Wanda loved the track and spent many hours in her room just singing her heart out. It was then she realised that she had a voice and that something could make her happy. That was singing.

On the day of the audition, Wanda had to argue with the conscience on her two shoulders. Should she or shouldn't she. She managed to walk to the Drama department and saw about six people outside the studio. Each of them were inconspicuous ordinary kids. She walked forward and then walked away. She did this three times until Suzy saw her and stopped her.

'You'll be Ok, just give it a go,' Suzy said, 'It will be worth it I promise.'

No one had ever promised her anything ever. This young girl looked at her with honest eyes. The good conscience won and Wanda stayed in the queue. The other six students made their way in one by one. It was now Wanda's turn and she walked into the room and onto a small stage. In front of her was a table and there was a light shinning straight in her face. She couldn't see much, but heard a voice.

'Name?'

Wanda answered in a whisper.

'Louder!' the voice shouted.

'Wanda,' she said loudly.

'What are you singing?' the same voice asked without any sympathy for the young people nerves.

'What's it gonna be, by En Vogue.'

'Ok have you got a backing track or are you singing Acapella?' the voice asked.

Wanda had no idea what he was talking about, but she wasn't an idiot and answered 'Acapella' Hoping she had worked out that that meant no music.

Wanda took a deep breath and went for it, giving it her all.

She wasn't sure how many people were watching as the light was blinding her, but as she finished there was applause. This was the first time Wanda had ever got any good response for anything she had done. It hit her like a flame. This is what she had been looking for all her young life. It was as if that applause filled her heart for the first time. She was in the middle of that feeling when she heard the same voice say.

'Ok. Thank you. Watch out for the poster going up this afternoon, it will let you know if you've got in. Have you got any questions?' a male voice asked rather hurriedly.

Wanda squinted under the lights and put her hand over her eyes. She had no idea what to ask, so the easiest thing to do was say no.

'Ok, next please!' the voice shouted.

She realised she was dismissed and made her way outside where Suzy was waiting for her.

'You've got an amazing voice.' Suzy told her.

'Have I?' Wanda asked truthfully.

'Didn't you know that?' Suzy asked.

Wanda went on to tell her that she had never sung in public before and she didn't know where that voice came from, it just happened.

'I bet you get in.' Suzy said and added, 'The results will be up on the board by about three o'clock. I'll tell you what, I'll meet you here at a quarter past three at the end of school and I'll make a bet with you.'

'Ok,' said Wanda reluctantly, 'What's the bet?'

'I bet you get in and if I'm wrong I have to buy you an ice cream. If you do get in, you have to buy me an ice cream!'

Wanda thought quickly and wondered if she did get in how the hell would she get the money for an ice cream, but she didn't believe she would, so she would have to face that when and if it came.

The end of school arrived and Wanda was uncertain if she should even go and look. Some of her little gang of friends found out that she had auditioned and had repeatedly taken the mick out of her all day. Wanda could take it, living with a large family meant she was use to being the butt of jokes. So she though she may as well see if she had got in. She got to the Drama studio and saw Suzy outside with a big grin on her face.

'You owe me an ice cream!' she announced.

'I got in?' Wanda said amazed, 'I really got in?'

Suzy nodded and said, 'So now you owe me an ice cream.'

Wanda thought for a while and decided that honesty was going to be the easiest way out.

'I would buy an ice cream, but I haven't got any money.' Wanda said quickly and looked down embarrassed.

'That's Ok,' Suzy said, 'I've got enough for both of us.'

From that point on they were firm friends. Wanda attended the choir practice twice a week. Not one person in her family even asked what she was up to, so as no one asked, she didn't tell anyone. Wanda spent plenty of days explaining to her friends why she had joined the choir, plus why she had taken up with Suzy, her new friend. She created plenty of excuses, but in fact she just loved music and especially singing. Even though this was her first experience of singing, the choir gave her some kind of escape. Escape from the grudge of being poor, of not being able to compete with the latest phase of young people needs and wants. Plus she met other kids that didn't live the life she did, their parents had jobs and they just joined the choir because they wanted to. A far cry from her little gang of girls that thought they ruled the school. This choir was Wanda's turning point. She had something to focus on and a reason to come to school.

'Wow!' Andy said suddenly, 'I think you should write a book, your fans would love to hear that story.'

Wanda explained that that was the good part of the story.

'I'm afraid it only went downhill after that.'

Sandy refilled everyone's glass and asked her to carry on. They were all fascinated by her story. Plus they all hoped that eventually they would find out why she hated Helga so much and why Helga was blackmailing her.

'I think that's enough for now.' Wanda said, 'But how about I reciprocate. I'm not on set tomorrow, so why don't I treat everyone to lunch. Then I'll tell you the next bit of the story! I can't give too much away at once now can I?'

Sandy and Andy looked at each other and silently gave each other the nod, there was no way they were going to miss out on the next bit of the story.

Wanda suggested the Lo Lo's over on the French side. Tom said he would pick them all up so they could go in one car. They arranged it for noon as Wanda and Tom said thank you and made their way out.

As the door shut behind them Andy said to Sandy, 'I'm even more intrigued now. Where on earth does Helga fit into the story and what the hell is a Lo Lo?'

'I think we may find that one out tomorrow, now I'm chucking you out. It's time to go home.' Sandy said pushing Andy towards the door.

'Get some rest and come back here for eleven in the morning so we can call Lucas and tell him what we've been up to.'

Andy saluted and said, 'Ok boss, see you tomorrow.' He shut the front door behind him as he left.

Sandy sat down and pondered on the day. First the mad man on the motorbike, then being attacked by so called pirates and to top it off, entertaining one of the biggest pop stars in the world, in her own house. Wow! What a day, she thought.

Chapter 11

At exactly one minute to eleven there was a loud bang on Sandy's front door. Thinking it was Andy, Sandy shouted, 'Just a minute!'

She opened the door and outside was a frantic Alan, the driver. He walked in with haste and sat down with a strange look on his face. Suddenly he spurted out, 'I tink I know who murdered dat actress!' Sandy was going to correct him and say actor, but it didn't seem the right time, so she just sat next to him and said, 'Ok, tell me why you think that.'

He went on to tell her that he was driving Brian, Wanda's manager around that morning and then he stopped talking.

'Go on,' cajoled Sandy.

'I know I shouldn't have bin listening,' he said and then carried on after taking a breath, 'But it was hard not to. He was sitting just behind my driver's seat and he wasn't being quiet on de phone.'

At that point the front door opened. Alan went quiet and in walked Andy with a cheerful, 'Morning!'

Sandy put her fingers to her lips and motioned him to come over. As he sat down she added, 'Alan thinks he knows who murdered Helga.'

'Oh!' said Andy as he looked at Alan with anticipation.

'So, I was driving Wanda's manager Brian and he was on de phone. I don't know who he was talking to but he told dem, dat...'

'Go on,' pushed Sandy, 'It's OK, you're with friends.' She then thought that was the second time in two days she had said that to someone. She worried that she might start sounding like a car dealer or an estate agent and then realised both Andy and Alan were just staring at her.

'Sorry!' she appologised, 'I just went off in a world of my own, do carry on.'

Alan took a deep breath and carried on. 'He said to someone on the phone, 'I'll come up with de money. You didn't have to do dat did you? I would have paid it! It was a bit drastic, don't you tink!' So you can see why, I had to come and tell you.

Both Sandy and Andy sat in silence.

'Thank you so much for telling us Alan,' said Sandy first. 'I think the best thing to do is carry on as normal and leave us to find out what it means.'

Andy just sat there and nodded in agreement.

'But it could be dangerous, especially if someone has already died. You better be careful you two. You shouldn't really mess around with... evil people.'

Sandy reassured him, they would be ok and that they would keep him posted. He left muttering something and went on his way.

Andy started first as Sandy was deep in thought. He repeated what Alan said, even using his Caribbean accent.

'I'll come up with de money. You didn't have to do dat did you? I would have paid it! It was a bit drastic, don't you tink?'

Sandy laughed and said, 'That is a bit worrying, especially the bit, 'you didn't have to do that'. I wonder what he was on about?'

'I said he was dodgy, I think he has definitely got something to do with this. Especially if Helga was blackmailing Wanda, then he has a motive and the opportunity with Helga in that caravan on her own. Has he told the police where he was? I bet he hasn't. Bloody dodgy guy of you ask me.' Andy spouted.

'Look,' said Sandy, 'We don't know what any of it means, I think we should get back to our plan and then see if we can piece it all together. Can you put some pictures up on our wall of Wanda and Brian then I'll go and call Lucas, like we planned. Then it will be time to go and meet Wanda. I don't know about you, but I'm dying to find out the next part of the story. Afterwards we can decide what to do next. Ok?'

Andy nodded and muttered as he left the room to go and do the honours in the 'Murder room'. Sandy picked up her phone to call Lucas at exactly the same time as he called her. She answered it and proceeded to tell him snippets of information they had collected. She told him she was going out for lunch with Wanda and that Wanda was being blackmailed by Helga. She also mentioned that they were hoping to find out more about it at lunch. She didn't say anything about Alan and his over hearing that conversation, as she didn't know if it was important yet. She decided to keep Lucas happy by giving him small amounts of info that she was certain of, but not the info that was still very vague. Lucas was pleased to hear she had got herself inconspicuously inside and told her to keep going.

Sandy relayed the message to Andy who was just pinning pictures up on the board.

'Ok.' Sandy said, 'Tom should be here in a minute, are you ready?'

Andy stuck the last picture up and turned round, 'Ok, let's wait outside for him. It's such a beautiful day and I'm hungry, so I'm looking forward to eating.' Andy marched outside.

They weren't out there long before Tom picked them up. He was on his own and explained that he wanted to talk to them first before picking up Wanda.

'I just wanted to make sure that whatever Wanda says today, that you have got her back. She has had enough trouble in her young life. I've only been working with her for about a month, since this stalker started playing silly games. She's a bit of a loner because she has come up against too many people that want to earn off her, too many people that want to sell her stories.'

'All we want Tom is to find Helga's killer, I promise we are not after anything else.' Sandy told him and then added, 'That goes for both of us, all we need to know is if Helga was blackmailing Wanda and if she was, why? Also we've heard from a very reliable source that Brian is up to something unsavoury. We are not sure yet, if it has anything to do with the murder, we are on the lookout.'

Tom started driving and it was quiet for a while in the car until Andy said, 'Tom? Do you think Brian has something to do with Helga's murder?'

Tom gave a little laugh and said, 'I'm not sure. I know he has been a 'bad boy' in his time, but murder? I'm not sure. There is something going on though. Brain seems to be keeping well away from me and that's unusual. He doesn't like it that someone else is looking after Wanda, so it may just be control, but something is definitely up.'

They drove over to Simpson Bay and up Billy Folly Road, passed the Casino and up towards the hill. Nestled in a quiet street was a block of ten

Condo's called 'Son Risa'. Wanda was hidden away in these Condo's. Tom called Wanda on the mobile, or cell phone as they call it out here, and told her they were here and ready.

There was a wonderful view from high up and you could see the boats coming in and out from the Simpson Bay Bridge, the same route they did on their trip the day before. Sandy couldn't believe that she had nearly been there a week and what a week it had been. She felt as if she had taken St Maarten into her heart and she knew she would not want to leave when the time came.

Suddenly she remembered what Alan, the driver had said on her first night and she smiled to herself. 'You'll be hooked, everyone is' he said and he was right.

'Wakey wakey!' Andy said to her, 'You looked like you were in a trance.'

'Just thinking that I'm not going to want to leave this Island when the time comes.'

With that the door opened and in skipped Wanda.

'Morning!' she interrupted, 'Hope you are hungry, I'm looking forward to lunch.'

They made small talk all the way. It was a journey of about thirty minutes, which passed the Airport and went over to the French side.

Wanda asked them if they had been to the Lo Lo's yet. Andy confessed they had no idea what a 'Lo Lo' was and they all laughed.

Wanda explained that in the 17th Century the plantation owners set up kitchens for the slaves called Lo Lo's. Now in the 20th Century they are small outdoor kitchens with good local cheap food.

'Like burger vans.' Andy suggested and they all laughed.

They parked their car in the car park and followed Wanda to a group of what looked like temporary outdoor kitchens. Wanda knew exactly where she was going and as she was wearing dark sunglasses and a cap so no one knew who she was. They all followed her and watched her as she smiled to a waitress and was seated immediately. They sat on the beach side of the Lo Lo, where they looked out onto the most amazing view, even more fabulous that Sandy's patio view.

They ordered the food, made some more small talk and then Wanda said, 'So I'm guessing your waiting for the second installment of the life of Wanda?'

'Yep!' said Andy, 'Holding nothing back.'

'You're funny,' said Wanda, 'Nothing like being honest. Ok where was I up to?'

'You had just been accepted into the choir and your bully friends were bugging you.' Andy recalled.

Wanda laughed at how simple Andy made it sound and proceeded to tell the rest of her story.

She was now fifteen and a regular member of the choir. She often sang lead in concerts and competitions. Her so-called friends still teased her, but she spent more time with Suzy now than the old gang of kids. One night after school when she didn't have any choir practice, she was invited to a party. One of the kids that lived near her invited about twelve kids over as her parents were out for the night. Wanda didn't need to tell anyone where she was going because no one cared. She met her friends Daisy and Glynn at the local grocery store and they stood there and chatted for a while then started to walk to the party. When they arrived at the house Daisy was whispering to Glynn.

'What are you two whispering about?' Wanda asked them.

'We are having a bet.' Glynn told her.

'A bet about what?'

Glynn put her hand in her pocket and came back out with three little white pills and said, 'That you wouldn't take one of these with us, we've got one each.'

Wanda looked at the pills then at the girls. She didn't like saying no to a dare and no matter how many films she had seen about not saying yes to pills or talks she had had at school, what harm could one little pill like that do? She said to herself she would only do it once. She took the pill, or rather snatched it, and stuck it in her mouth and swallowed.

'That,' she said to her new friends around the lunch table, 'Was how it all started.'

As she finished her sentence the waitress came over holding all three plates and handed them over. They had all chosen fish and it looked delicious. They ate up and chatted idly until Andy asked Wanda to carry on with her story.

Wanda went on to say how that one little pill started the ball rolling and by the time she was in her final year at school, she spent most of it high and didn't remember much about it at all. As she didn't have any spare cash, she found genius ways of getting it. Mostly stealing from anyone or anywhere.

Just after she turned sixteen she got caught with a bag of pills and got arrested for dealing. Wanda recollected that first night in the cell of the police station. How it felt to be all alone in the dark and know that she had got herself here and no one was going to come and get her, because no one cared. Her mother had gone AWOL, the kids hadn't seen her for days and her brothers and sisters had left the house. Wanda was truly on her own.

The next morning she found herself in the court in front of a magistrate. She knew from her barrister who visited her early in the morning that getting arrested with a bag of twenty-two pills meant a prison sentence. So, she expected the worse. The whole court case seemed to be over in a flash. She was given a twelve-month sentence but it would be deferred if she went straight into rehab. Her barrister recommended that she told the judge she would go that night, so she did. That was where she met Tamara, Helga's daughter.

At that point, Sandy raised her eyebrows and thought 'so that's it, in rehab with Helga's daughter, but I wonder why she would blackmail her? Plenty of young people go into rehab and still move forward. There must be another part of the story' and turned back to listen.

Wanda said, 'Are you sure you want to hear more? I'm happy to stop there if you've had enough.'

'And leave it at a good bit? Come on, let's hear it warts and all, as they say.' Andy pleaded.

Wanda talked about how she felt that first night in rehab and as she had been on pills for nearly two years every day taking more and more, she was thin, grey looking, angry and aggressive. So different from the girl in the choir aged thirteen. She knew she had to get off them but she felt at that point she had no reason to live.

They had put her in her own single room and on the first afternoon at one o'clock a girl turned up at her door and poked her head round and said shyly, 'Hello!' She had a posh voice and introduced herself as Tamara. I hadn't ever met a girl like her. She came into my room and talked to me. She talked to me all night to take away the pain I was feeling from withdrawing from the drugs. She told me all about her mother who didn't care about her and sent her away to school or with nannies. She told me about the nanny that died and I felt so sorry for her. She sat there talking to me a bit like I'm talking to you now, just unloading everything, but there was one big difference between us and that was money. She came from a wealthy background where money bought you anything you needed and I came from the other side of town.

We quickly became firm friends, but I didn't realise that she wasn't trying to get clean. She was self destructive and just playing a game with everyone. I was totally the opposite, I never wanted to land back up in that court again and I never wanted to sleep in a cell in a police station again ever! One night she came to see me and she made up a story about how she needed to go home and get some pictures that meant everything to her. I believed her and together we managed to evade the staff and get out the back door, through the gardens and over the fence. At the time, I just saw it as a laugh. In my mind we weren't doing anything wrong, she was just going home to pick up some pictures. Unbeknown to me, Tamara was actually after cash and she knew where her mum kept it and she knew no one was at home. I was her stooge.

We climbed the fence and ran, I followed her and we managed to get a taxi buy telling them we were going to pick up some money, I just listened. Silly really but I was only sixteen and not very worldly. We travelled to Wansted, an up market East London town. It wasn't far from Walthamstow, but far enough. The houses changed to a big Edwardian style that I thought then, were mansions. I had never been anywhere except on a coach to a choir competition.

Tamara knew that the spare key was hidden in the tiny front garden under a fake stone. She got it out as I stood watching amazed that someone could hide something in such a ridiculous place, but I followed her as she opened the door and went inside. She told me to wait downstairs in what I guessed was the living room. To me it looked like something out of a film set, it had the most beautiful furniture, not a thing out of place and on the wall above the fireplace was a big picture of a woman. Now I know it was Helga, but then I just saw the beautiful woman looking at me with amazing blue eyes.

Wanda seemed to come out of her trance and said, 'This was the start of Helga's evil ways.'

'Evil? That doesn't sound like the Helga I knew. She just seemed rather innocent and easy going.'

Wanda laughed and carried on, 'We got caught as Tamara didn't know about the new alarm system. The police came and called Helga who arrived within thirty minutes. She talked to the police and then they left. I've never been so worried and she had one little talk and 'puff' our problem disappeared. She sent Tamara to her room and I was left with her. She told me she was taking me back to the rehab centre and that I must never talk about this event ever again. I just stood there and nodded. She was the most beautiful woman I had ever seen and the most powerful. I had seen her on television and to see her in front of me now made me rather reticent. I knew I had to go back so I just said, 'What will they do to me?'

'Nothing.' She replied. 'I'll tell them I took you both out for a coffee and Tamara doesn't want to come back. They won't argue with me.'

'With that, she picked up her car keys and took me back.'

She came back into my life again about four weeks ago, when she knew that The Helter Skelter was being axed. Sandy's eyes lifted as she heard this comment. So Helga knew at least four weeks ago that our job was over. Wow, she was a sly one.

Wanda continued, 'She came and asked me to see if I could get her cast as my mother on this film. I told her I had nothing to do with the casting and she wouldn't leave it there. She bought up how she knew who I really was and that I was a fraud and she would tell everyone if I didn't try and get her cast. So you can see, she wasn't my best friend and I can't blame who ever it was that killed her, but one thing I know for sure it wasn't me. Evenutally I got clean and even went back to school to take my exams. Just after I left school I filmed myself on Suzy's iPad singing and we put it on YouTube. From There my story is public knowledge. I got a record deal a manager and…'

'Was That Brian?' Andy butted in.

'No, his name was Simon. He was my manager for just over a year.' Wanda said.

'What happened to him?' Andy asked.

Wanda laughed and said, 'You're bloody nosey aren't you!'

'I'm sorry, was that over the mark. It's just so fascinating, not like my boring life. If you ever want to write your memoirs, I'll ghost write for you,' he offered.

Wanda laughed again and carried on telling her tale.

'Simon was not the perfect manager that everyone thought, he was a bit too hands on. Eventually I reported him to the record company and they said they would get me a new one, then Brian turned up.'

'Turned up? That's a strange explanation.' Sandy said.

Wanda explained that Brian had been her dealer. He had supplied me with drugs for the two years that I was hooked. He then went through something very similar to me and he begged me to give him a chance when the rest of the world wouldn't and that is how and why Brian is so protective. He knows how easy it is to slip back into a life of crime and how hard it is to stay clean. So, that's my story!'

Sandy thanked Wanda for her honesty and asked her, 'So that's why you disliked her so much and did you get her the job as your mother?'

'That's the funny thing. She didn't need to blackmail me because her name was already up for consideration, but they thought she was under contract with The Helter Skelter. So when I mentioned to casting that the show was ending, they did all the work and she was cast.'

'So Helga got the job on her own merit. Do you have any idea who might have killed her?'

'Nope!' Wanda answered, 'At first I considered that Brian might have had something to do with it, as he knew about Helga and our little secret, but I'm sure he didn't.' Wanda finished when Andy added, 'What makes you so sure?'

'I don't know, just instinct.' She mused.

'Wanda?' Sandy asked, 'Would you be able to help us?'

'Help doing what?'

Sandra and Andy started to tell Wanda that they were working with Lucas the Chief of Police and that they had been asked to find out what they could about Helga's murder.

Wanda suddenly looked sad, 'So, this was all pretense? You weren't interested in me, but wanted to know if I had something to do with the murder of Helga?'

Andy said, 'I promise you Wanda, we are true honest people, but I have a confession to make. Please don't be angry with us, if it's time for confessions, I need to confess something.'

Wanda looked on with a stern look and Sandra crossed her fingers behind her back hoping desperately he wasn't going to mention the reporter he pretended to be to interview her. That would mean Wanda losing faith completely.

'I'm a...Fan! I've always been since your first single,' he spluttered out, 'So when Tom suggested dinner, I was the one that said yes please. Look let's start again. We are all in the same boat. We are all on a Caribbean island and we don't know anyone, so for the next eleven weeks at least we can spend some of that time together. We promise we are harmless.'

Sandy nodded in agreement just thankful that was all he said. For the first time, Tom added something to the conversation, up until now he had kept very quiet.

'Sandy has a point Wanda, at least spending time with these two will be a lot better than spending time shut away, like you have been. How about getting involved, that might be interesting, you could help them with their enquiries.'

Wanda's face lit up, 'Me, a detective?'

'We are not exactly detectives Wanda, were just helping. I don't want you to get the wrong idea. All we do is ask questions really and feed back the information,' confirmed Sandy.

'Oh well! If it not dangerous.' Wanda said and then added, 'I'm only joking. Making films can be really hard work, too much down time. I'll be happy to help, when do we start?'

Sandy was going to invite them back to her Condo and show them the 'Murder Room' but remembered the only pictures up on the board were of Wanda and Brian, so maybe not.

'How about now!' Andy added, 'We need to find out where Brian was at the time of the murder, so we can rule him out.'

From Makeup to Murder

Well done Andy, thought Sandy, straight to the point.

'How am I going to do that, accept for asking him straight out and then he could lie?'

'I know,' said Andy, 'Let's all go out for dinner tonight and see what happens, does he like men or women?' he asked.

Wanda laughed and said, 'I think its women.'

'Ok, Sandy, then it's up to you to use your female wiles.'

'What am I going to do? Tickle him until he tells me?' Sandy asked.

They all roared with laughter and Andy said, 'You'll think of something. Now! Where shall we meet? How about going to Cherie's in Maho?'

With that Wanda called Brian and said he just had to meet her new friends and arranged for them all to meet at half past seven at Cherie's.

'Well done,' said Andy, 'Your first job is completed. You're going to be good at this!'

'If they are all as easy as that,' Wanda said, 'I'll be fabulous!'

Tom called for the bill and though he did try and pay for it, they all insisted on paying for themselves.

They walked back to the car park and settled themselves into the car. They idly chatted all the way back and Tom dropped Sandy and Andy off first and then drove on to take Wanda home. Andy followed Sandy up the steps to her Condo and went inside with her.

'Wow!' Sandy said, 'I need a minute to take it all in!'

'At least we can take Wanda's picture off of the wall. We know it wasn't her,' Andy added.

Both of them sat down and were silent just for a minute.

'Wanda really opened up for us didn't she?' Andy said.

'We must look honest,' said Sandy.

'I felt bad really, getting her to believe we just wanted to be friends when all we wanted was to make sure she wasn't our murderer,' Andy murmured.

'But look what's happened, she is now on our side and working with us, how good is that?'

Chapter 12

Cherie's, the restaurant they picked, wasn't far from Sandy's place, so Andy got a taxi to hers and then they walked together. At exactly seven o'clock they got to the outdoor colourful exterior and waited for the Maître D'. He strolled over casually and Sandy could see his label on his shirt said 'Mohamed'.

'Good evening Mohamed, we have a table booked for five people at seven o'clock,' she said. Sandy thought to herself that she wasn't sure what name the table was booked under.

'I think it's booked under Tom,' she started with. Mohamed looked in his book and said, 'Perfect, I have the best table ready for you right near the stage.'

Whoops Sandy thought to herself, Wanda may not like that as I'm sure she prefers to stay anonymous, but just followed Mohamed and thought they should wait until the others get here before asking to change. They sat down and ordered drinks and within five minutes the others arrived. Wanda was wearing a maxi dress, her long hair was tied up on top of her head and she wore sunglasses. Tom was behind her and then Brian.

Brian was a stocky tall guy in his late twenties who looked like he had been in a fight or two. He looked like a man not to be messed with. He was wearing jeans and flip-flops with a smart white shirt on. His hair was very short and he had sunglasses on top of his head, even though it was evening and the sun had gone in about two hours ago. Wanda introduced Sandy and Andy to Brain and they all sat down. Wanda maneuvered it so that Brian was sitting next to Sandy and Wanda was next to Andy and Tom. Mohamed came over and passed around five large menu's and the three of them ordered some drinks.

Andy spoke first by asking, 'Have you been here before?' They each shook their head in a no and Tom said, 'I've heard lots about it though, it seems they have a floor show later.'

'Good!' said Wanda. It will be nice to watch someone else perform for a change.'

They all chose their food and gave their orders to Mohamed, not sure why the Maitre D' had become their waiter, but it was probably because of Wanda being with them.

They all chatted away as Sandy started to work on Brian. At first they just made small talk and he seemed a pleasant sort of guy and certainly not as aggressive as he first looked. He told her how he loves looking after Wanda and he couldn't imagine doing anything else. Sandy gave him a quick rundown of her life on the soap 'The Helter Skelter' and then being whisked away to the Caribbean.

It was Brian that started talking about Helga first and commented on what a shock it must have been to find the lifeless body. Well he didn't actually say lifeless body, but that's what he meant and because he bought up the subject she felt like it was now open for debate and she got stuck in.

'It was a shock,' Sandy said, 'I've worked with Helga for such a long time, that to see her like that was awful. Plus it was the first time I've ever seen a dead body. Have you ever seen a dead body Brian?' She waited for a reply. Brian was not shy and shared his story with her.

'I've seen too many in my life,' he said telling her all about it. Brian had grown up in Walthamstow near Wanda and just like her he came from a mixed up broken family. In fact he said he wasn't even sure how many brothers and sisters he had as his loser father would come in and out of his life often bringing other woman into the picture. He learnt to be tough at a young age and was always a leader not a follower. This meant he saw his far share of fights and squabbles and although he stayed out of the local gangs he saw a multitude of sins including battles with knives and even guns. So yes, he had seen dead bodies.

He couldn't wait to get out of his way of life, but one thing was stopping him and that was money. At the age of fifteen he started to sell cigarettes to the school kids. He would go to the local cash and carry and bluff them that he was buying for his fictitious father's sweet shop and then make a nice profit at school. That was how it started, with cigarettes, which progressed on to drugs. Brian was quite happy to tell Sandy everything, holding nothing back. They were still deep in conversation when the food came.

'I'd love to hear the rest, maybe you could carry on the story later?' Sandy said to Brain.

The food was delicious and there was so much of it. Just as they finished their food the floorshow started. First to come out was an older guy who had trouble walking so he sat on a high chair. Next to him was a guy with a large keyboard and sound equipment. They sang a few classic songs and then a large Caribbean gentleman dressed as a very large banana came out. He sang the most hilarious suggestive song Sandy had ever heard. They all laughed and that set the scene for the remainder of the evening. The next guy that came out was dressed as Tina Turner with the highest heels Sandy had ever seen. He was athletic, a great dancer and vocalist. What he could do in high heels was amazing.

At one point they asked for audience participation and Andy jumped up put his hand in the air with an urgency and tried to get someone else from the table to join him, but all he was met with was 'no way' so he went up all on his own.

They found about six men to volunteer and put grass skirts and coconut bras on each of them. They looked ridiculous, but then that was the intention. Andy loved the attention and when they set the volunteers the task of twerking, he gave it his all. They decided the winner by applause and when it came to Andy's turn the whole table stood up and roared along with the rest of the restaurant. The winner was unanimous and Andy was awarded a bottle of cheap champagne. He came back to the table to a round of applause, which he lapped up. He was truly in his element.

They congratulated Andy and Wanda said, 'I think maybe you have missed your vocation, do you fancy joining my dancers for my next tour?'

Andy took this with a pinch of salt but added, 'I shall look forward to it!'

They decided not to have dessert where they were, but to go onto the Ice Cream Parlour in Simpson Bay. They all piled into Tom's car and off they went. The Ice Cream Parlour in Simpson Bay was in a huge building that housed an original Italian Carousel. It was always busy and they all trooped in and chose an Ice Cream and sat down to eat it.

'Thank you guys, for such a great evening, it's been a long time since I've had a normal evening, without even being approached and I can't tell you how that makes me feel.' Wanda said.

Andy suggested, 'Let's go back to Sandy's for a coffee!'

They all laughed and looked at Sandy. 'Sure,' she said and they all got back in to Tom's car.

They started driving along Simpson Bay and Tom said, 'Don't look behind guys, but do any of you know someone with a black Toyota? I'm sure we are being followed.'

'No!' they all said in unison.

'Do you think it's my stalker?' Wanda asked.

'No.' Tom answered, 'This guy is much older. Hold on tight guys, I'm going to lose him.'

With that Tom did a skilful u-turn and waited to see if the black Toyota followed, but he didn't.

'False alarm,' he told them as they all settled back in to their seats.

'I thought we were being followed the other day.' Sandy said, 'When we were in Philipsburg,' she added.

'I thought I saw someone lurking around on the film set when I...' Andy was about to say impersonating a reporter and realised he couldn't, 'When I was clearing up some of Helga's things,' he improvised instead.

'Are you sure?' Tom asked.

'No, that's why I didn't say anything,' said Sandy

'Me too!' added Andy, 'I just thought I was being paranoid.'

'That's what I thought too!' added Sandy.

'Ok guys. You have got to be careful, if you are being followed its very likely to not be good. You must tell the Chief of Police and let him get some security for you. Maybe you've been asking too many people too many questions.'

'Am I missing out on something here?' Brian asked.

Wanda said, 'These two are just nosey and ask lots of questions about everything,' putting him off the scent.

With that Tom turned the car back round again and they made their way to Sandy's place.

Chapter 13

As they walked into Sandy's Tom, Wanda and Andy disappeared quickly onto the patio. Brian helped Sandy with making the coffees. Sandy could just see the three of them peaking through the patio doors and giggling trying to see what she was doing. They looked a bit like the three little pigs in a cartoon looking into the brick house. As Brian had his back to her, she signaled to them to go away just as Brian turned round to see what she was doing. To try and cover up she said, 'Blasted mosquito's they get everywhere.' Waving her arms around. Brian said nothing but gave her an odd look as she carried on trying to swat an imaginary mosquito. Sandy took the coffees outside to the three stooges and as she came back in Wanda closed the patio door leaving the two of them inside.

Brian looked on astonished and shook his head as if to say 'what the hell are those three doing' but Sandy broke the moment by asking him to carry on with his story and motioned for him to sit down.

'Where did I get up to?' Brian asked and then added, 'Are you sure you want to hear? It's a bit boring honestly.'

'Look, I've spent the last fifteen years in one job going to one place every day. Everybody else's life is far more interesting than mine I assure you.' Sandy said as she took a sip of coffee and checked the nutters at the patio had given up watching, which they had and were now all deep in conversation.

'Ok.' Brian said and carried on with his story.

Brian was rather successful in his school shop, each day his shop would open at break-time and cigarettes and sweets were his stock. By the time he was sixteen and had to start thinking about what he would do when he left school. His only real experience and want was to sell. Brian didn't like school and for the last year he wasn't there much at all, he was happy to get out as soon as possible. Near his house was a corner shop and he had visited it since he was a child. Mr Patel, the owner knew him well and knew what he had been up to at school, with his little shop. So, one day he stopped Brian and said, 'Do you want a job?' Just like that.

Brian was shocked and agreed immediately and started at six o'clock the next morning. Brian watched everything and learnt fast. He was like a sponge and realised very quickly that he wanted to be in business. But he was greedy and about six months down the line he saw one of his friends making big money. He asked him about it and was told that he made his money selling Marijuana and pills. He was also told 'never take the stuff yourself, that's where people go wrong, just sell to the rich kids and keep the profit'.

So Brian became a dealer and he admitted that was where he met Wanda. He suddenly said, 'I know she has told you her story.'

Sandy was a bit surprised that Wanda had told him this, but said nothing and listened as he carried on. He told Sandy that his job didn't last much longer as Mr Patel caught him selling to a teenager. He bollocked him and sent him out saying, 'You'll never make anything of yourself you stupid idiot. Grow up and be a man, not a vial human being, you're sacked. Come back when you've changed your ways.'

Brian confessed he was young and stupid and thought he knew better, but to keep up his life style he took his trade to the back streets of Walthamstow, until he got caught.

Brian got caught the first time at the age of seventeen. He was only given a warning as he managed to get rid of the stuff just as the police got hold of him. He evaded getting arrested until he was nineteen and he knew immediately that his only way out was to get straight. He spent twelve months in a Detention Centre in West London narrowly missing being charged as an adult and escaping a term in prison. He emerged after his incarceration with a string of A Levels and a chance to change his life for the better.

At the age of twenty three Brian had taken a degree in Business Studies and was eager to take on a business of his own. Brain read in the newspaper that Wanda had just sacked her manager and he took a chance and hoped she would take a chance on him. He wrote her a letter, telling her the same story as he had just told Sandy and she listened and she gave him a chance.

'That's it,' he said, 'That's my story. I've been managing her for four and a half years now and I love it.'

At that point Wanda opened the patio doors and said, 'I think it's time to come in we are being bitten alive out here.'

'Come and join us.' Sandy said, 'Brian has been telling me his life story. Boy! Between the pair of you, you two have enough to make your own blockbuster film.'

The evening broke up and Tom took Wanda and Brian home. They agreed to do it again another night as the evening was so much fun. As the door shut behind them and they left Andy asked hurriedly, 'Well? Did he do it?'

Sandy just laughed and said, 'I've no idea, but I don't think so. He seems a nice guy and he has had hard times. He seems to have learnt from it though. I can't see murder is in his nature.'

'But, maybe he got someone else to do it for him?' Andy suggested.

'I just can't see it. He has worked so hard to get this job, I'm sure he wouldn't jeopardize it. We do need to find out where he was at the time of the murder though,' Sandy Said.

'Why don't you just ask him?' Andy said shrugging his shoulders. 'Why haven't the police asked him that? I thought they had spoken to everyone involved.'

'I think that's the problem, they don't think he is involved. It's only us that knows Helga was blackmailing Wanda and although it was dealt with because she got the job on the film, they don't know there was bad blood between them. Even if Helga had told the world about Wanda's time in rehab, who would care? It's not a reason to murder.'

'Mmmm,' said Andy, 'If Brian doesn't have anything to do with Helga's death then we have run out of suspects. Where do we go next?'

'I think we should tell Lucas in the morning what we have found out so far. Even the blackmailing and get them to talk to Brian and find out where he was. He is less likely to lie to the police and at least they can check his alibi. Also I'm a bit suspicious about this man we have both seen, something isn't right,' Sandy replied.

They both were surprised when Sandy's mobile went 'ding'. She read the text message and relayed it's contents to Andy.

'We've both been invited for lunch tomorrow at Bamboo Bernies in Maho by Wanda and Brian.'

'I know where that is, I went there with Helga the first night we arrived,' said Andy, 'It's a Fab restaurant,' he added enthusiastically.

So they ended their evening with Andy leaving and a plan for lunch the next day.

The next morning was Saturday and Sandy was doing all her household chores. She didn't do much as each time she started a task she got too hot and gave up. The morning went quickly and at about eleven o'clock she decided to call Lucas to give him an update. As soon as he answered the phone she said, 'Hi Lucas, we have had a few busy days.'

Sandy proceeded to tell him what they had been up to. How they had befriended Wanda and found out all about her past and how Helga was connected, but assured him that Wanda wasn't the murderer and explained why. She then went on to talk about Brian and how she was sure he wasn't the murderer either, but they haven't yet asked him where he was at the time of the murder.

'Ah!' said Lucas, 'We know the answer to that. It seems he has a passion for gambling and he was at a private poker game that went on from eleven in the evening until ten in the morning, so he has an alibi.'

'Good!' said Sandy, 'I really didn't want it to be him.'

Then Sandy started to talk about the stranger she saw and how Tom thought they were being followed.

Lucas cut in with, 'Tom called me last night and told me everything. I'm happy that you are going out to lunch and that he will be with you today. I'll make sure that when you leave lunch I will have someone discreetly watching and keeping you safe. It's obvious that whoever is watching you, knows you are asking questions, so my advice is to cool off and leave the rest to us now.'

Sandy thanked him and said she would keep in touch. She went into the 'Murder Room' and removed the remaining pictures and all that was left was the single picture of Helga. Sandy suddenly felt sad, on two counts. She sat down in the room and thought first about her long-term colleague who had died and secondly that she hadn't solved the murder and was no nearer than the day Helga died.

Sandy hadn't let herself grieve or feel the pain. She had been so engrossed with finding out who did it that this was the first time she had taken a moment and truly thought about it. She thought about her future too. Sandy loved her job, but now she didn't have a regular gig and that felt scary. Plus she had seen a little of paradise and St Maarten had spurned her to travel more. Luckily the world of filmmaking stretched all around the world, so maybe if the production company here liked her she may get to go travelling a lot further than she thought.

She had heard that the next film they were making was a remake of 'Cleopatra' and their next destination was Egypt.

Sandy sat and pondered for about half an hour until there was a knock on the door. She shook herself back to life and went to open the door to Andy. He noticed her demeanor and questioned it.

'Are you OK?' he asked.

'I've just been sitting thinking,' she answered.

'Did it hurt?' he asked facetiously, but realised very quickly that she was serious, so he appologised and tried to make light of it.

Sandy explained how she felt and that she was hopeful for the future, but she felt a bit deflated that all their enquires had come to nothing and they didn't seem to be any nearer to finding out who murdered Helga than they were five days ago! Andy agreed but reminded her that what they had done was important and that between the pair of them they had discounted all the suspects and that without their detective work that may not have happened. Sandy took it all in and smiled.

'True!' she suddenly said, 'If it wasn't for us, the police would not have known and discounted Guy and his wife. Or Wanda and Brian. That's all down to us.'

'Ok!' Andy uttered, 'We have a lunch appointment to attend to and it's time to leave.'

Sandy smiled picked up her car keys and they left to make their way to Maho and Bamboo Bernies. It wasn't far, but it was too hot today and they didn't fancy walking. They drove through the single narrow land between the beach and the airport fence, past all the silly tourists standing just waiting for the larger planes to take off and throw them about or trying to get a good picture of a plane coming in and nearly touching them as they stand on the beach wall. No one took any notice of the large sign saying:

'Jet blast of departing and arriving Aircraft can cause severe physical harm resulting in extreme bodily harm and/or death!'

Even though Sandy had not been on the Island long she had quickly noticed that every day there were hundreds of idiots trying to cause extreme bodily harm to themselves and pretend they can't read. Hundreds of tourists came off cruise boats just to perform this ridiculous procedure every day. In fact Sandy had got so fed up with them, she felt like flicking their ankles as she drove past and could actually easily do it as they stood so near the cars and selfishly just waited to be blasted. Most of them try to take a video of the whole event so that they can upload them to You Tube along with millions of others. In fact the airport boasts it as one of the top three dangerous landings in the world and is frequently appearing in Documentaries.

They eventually got through the crowds and drove the short distance to the underground car park.

The barriers came up to let them in and unnoticed by either of them, they were followed in by a black Toyota. Sandy went up to the first floor and pulled into a parking space opposite an exit at the same time the Black Toyota pulled behind them quickly blocking them in. Neither of them saw it happen but heard the sound of the wheels on the tarmac. They both were a bit stunned as the driver jumped out and opened Sandy's door with such a force that she automatically shouted, 'What the...' But didn't have time to finish as she saw a gun pointing straight into her face.

Andy just sat there and froze, he couldn't get a single word out and before Sandy could utter anything they were told to get out of their car and into the Toyota, by a gruff voice. They both obeyed without saying a word. Having a gun pointed straight at you makes you do as the gunman says pretty quickly without question, so the pair of them found out.

The gunman was in his mid fifties, clean-shaven, but worn looking as if he had lived a hard life. He was wearing jeans and a non-discreet t-shirt. He had the look of anger and evil in equal shares in his eyes. He was the man Sandy had spotted at the photo shop and Andy had seen on the set, but that did not help at all.

'Get in the back!' he shouted and closed the door after pushing them both in one side.

'You can't get out!' he said as he got in the driver's seat, 'Don't make a noise, it won't take long for me to turn round and shoot, so don't try it.' He continued menacingly and both believed him wholeheartedly and realised this wasn't the time to be clever or witty. This guy meant business and they knew it.

Chapter 14

Two things happened at precisely the same moment that Sandy and Andy were forced into the black Toyota.

The first was Sandy's mobile phone started to ring and as she couldn't answer it, it went straight to answer phone. The caller left this message,

'Hi Sandy, It's Lucas. I needed to tell you that we have received some forensic information about Helga's murderer. It seems your worry about that car following you was correct. We have found DNA of a man called Philip Jorden and that car is his rental car. He went to school with Helga and he has spent most of his life in and out of jail. I am guessing that he is Helga's murderer, but we are not sure why yet. We think he is extremely dangerous and he knows you've been asking questions. I'm going to call Tom to tell him the info, but for now stick with Tom and stay where you are until I can get someone to you. Call me and let me know where you are and that you are safe.'

At the exact same time, Tom, Wanda and Brian were at Bamboo Bernies and Tom had become suspicious that Sandy hadn't arrived, as she was always so punctual. He picked up his mobile and called Sandy too. It just rang and he said to the other two, 'That's strange there is no answer.'

'Try her again, maybe she was driving and it's only five minutes after twelve,' Wanda suggested innocently.

Tom tried again just as Lucas was trying to call him.

'Nope!' he said and added, 'It's gone to answer phone, there is something niggling me, I'm suspicious. That's not like them to be unreachable. If Sandy was driving then Andy would answer the phone. I need to do something. I can't just sit here. I'm going to make some calls.' Tom stood up and made his way out of the restaurant. He looked out onto Maho streets from his advantage point high up in Maho shops and suddenly saw the black Toyota coming out of the underground car park very fast. Like a flash he ran into the car park and immediately saw Sandy's car with the two front doors left open and no sign of them. He thought quickly and made a call to Lucas. As Lucas answered he heard him say, 'I've been trying to get hold of you.'

'We have a problem,' Tom said, 'I'm standing by Sandy and Andy's car and the doors are wide open and they are not here. I think they have been taken forcibly.'

Lucas told Tom the information he left on Sandy's answer phone about Philip Jorden, but added one thing extra.

'Tom I think this man is likely to be armed and dangerous, Sandy and Andy are in trouble. It looks like he has been working at Bamboo Bernies as a waiter if you...'

Tom butted in with, 'I just saw the black Toyota that was following us last night, it came out of the car park only minutes ago. I bet that was him with Sandy and Andy.'

'Ok!' Lucas answered, 'We are on our way. Wait there for us we won't be long.'

Meantime Wanda and Brian were completely unaware of what was going on and were debating whether they should order lunch or wait for them all to return. Little did they know, that might never happen.

By now Sandy and Andy realised the enormity of the situation and they were both panicked. Sandy looked into the drivers mirror to take in the kidnappers features to her memory and deep in her brain she recollected a phrase, 'Stockholm Syndrome' where captors befriend their kidnapper in order to get a safe conclusion. So she tried to make conversation by saying, 'Where are you taking us?' 'Shut the fuck up!' he grunted and added, 'Don't worry you'll hear it all, the whole bloody story, before I kill you both.'

That made Andy shiver and Sandy looked at him with reassuring eyes. Sandy looked at the route they were taking and made sure she saved it in her memory. They drove through the golf course at Mullet Bay, past the Casino and towards Cupecoy.

At Maho Tom ran back to Wanda and Brian and told them hurriedly that Sandy and Andy had been taken forcibly by Helga's murderer and they were now waiting for the police to arrive. He called over the head waiter and asked him, 'Does a Philip Jorden work here?'

'Who's asking?' the waiter said.

'The Police!' Tom bluffed, 'And this is now a matter of life or death, so I suggest you answer quickly and correctly. Does Philip Jorden work here?' he repeated with authority.

'He does,' he answered, 'But he is not in today. We haven't seen him for a few days. He is a strange guy, doesn't say much.'

'Do you have an address for him,' he asked obviously in a hurry.

'I'll check.' He left to go into the restaurant office.

Wanda came up and asked, 'What can we do?'

'Nothing at the moment.' Tom said and followed the waiter into his office.

'That address,' he said gruffly, 'Quickly, come on, where is it?'

The man was fumbling in an old filling cabinet and turned round with a scrap of paper.

'That's all I've got,' he said and passed it over.

Tom took the scrap of paper and turned round and left the office. He walked back to Brian and said, 'Look I think us three will go to this address and see what we can find. When the police get here, which should be any minute, they will want to follow the route the black Toyota went off in, so let's get into the car park and start from there.' He passed the scrap of paper over to Wanda to keep hold off.

As soon as they left and started walking to the car park, they heard sirens and three police pulled up around Sandy's car. Lucas walked out and Tom went over to speak to him. He told them that the black Toyota turned left and made its way through Mullet bay, that's all he could see.

Lucas went over to the other police officers gathering and gave out instructions. One car left in a hurry and two officers stayed to deal with the forensics whilst Lucas and his driver left to go back to the station to work from there. Tom had neglected to tell Lucas that he had an address for Philip Jorden.

'You didn't say anything about this address,' Wanda said holding the scrap of paper out.

'No,' he answered, 'I wanted us to do that ourselves. If we have any chance of saving Sandy and Andy, we need to do it inconspicuously and the Island Police are not that. We stand more chance of helping them than they do.'

'Ok,' said Brian and Wanda simultaneously and followed Tom over to his car. They all got in and Tom put the details in his satnav and off they went.

'It says the place we are looking for is over the hill and should take us about twenty minutes. Buckle up guys, I'm going to try and make it as fast as I can,' Tom said as he drove off at break neck speed.

The driver, with Sandy and Andy in the back, pulled the car over a rough bit of ground and told the pair of them to stay where they were and got out. He opened the boot and got a large piece of old tarpaulin out. He then opened Sandy door and ordered her to get out and then Andy. He threw this old cover over the car and told the two of them in a really menacing way, 'I'm taking you to somewhere no one will find you. You'll walk where I tell you and no trying to be clever. I'll have a gun pointed at your back. Don't forget that! Now go straight ahead and walk down to the beach.'

Sandy started walking over the rough terrain and Andy followed. The pair of them said nothing, as it was hard to know what to say. They were both just terrified.

'Hurry up!' Their assailant shouted at them and they tried to move faster. They eventually made it over the rough terrain and onto the beach. Sandy could see ahead there was a cave and guessed that was where they were being taken to.

'Hurry up!' He shouted again and motioned for them to go over to the rocky wall that protected the beach from the cliffside. 'See that cave over there?' he asked, 'That's going to be your new home for a while, maybe a very long while!'

Andy took a sneak peek behind and was told to turn around and look where he was going. They came to the cave and stopped.

As Sandy and Andy arrived at the cave, Tom, Wanda and Brian arrived at the address on the scrap of paper. They were in a district that was not on the main drag, but down a back street with lots of young local youths hanging about on the street corners. Wanda felt conspicuous and put on her sunglasses and her peaked cap pulled down low. She always kept one in her bag for when she didn't want to be recognised and this was definitely one of those times. They were now parked outside a one-story house that looked like it needed some work. The shutters were worn with some missing and the front garden was a jungle of weeds, not like the neat houses on either side. Tom asked Brian to look after Wanda as he was going in to see if anyone was at home.

He left the car and shut the door carefully. He walked slowly up the path taking a look each way in case he was discovered and as he reached the front of the house he looked in the front window. There were no lights on. He took something out of his pocket, looked around and using a small metal object opened the lock on the door. The door opened and Tom pushed it slightly. Nothing could be heard and it was dark. Like in the movies, Tom stood sideways and walked like a crab into the house. After five minutes Tom came outside and motioned for Brain and Wanda to come in. Brian got our first and asked, 'Are you sure it is safe for Wanda to be here?'

Tom wasn't sure if he was worried more about Wanda or himself, but assured them that he had checked the house and no one was in. Plus he was very unlikely the man was going come back as he would realise someone would find out where he lives.

All three of them walked through the front door at the same time Philip Jorden had finished tying up Sandy and Andy's feet and arms with some rope in the cave. He then put tape over their mouths. This in particular pissed Sandy off, she didn't like not being able to talk.

Sandy looked around her and saw they had been led into a small cave. They were about twenty foot inside the entrance and although it was quite small they could still see the sea. It was quite dark and cool and very scary. Inside the cave the rocks opened into a small circular section, which was about six foot in height and fifteen foot in diameter, so although their captor had sat them down he nearly reached the top of the cave with his height. Next to the spot they sat in was the remains of what Sandy thought were John's belongings. A small, tired and worn sports bag, a blanket, pillow and some part eaten food and a small wooden stool.

Sandy wondered how long he had been hiding out here for and how evil he really was. All of a sudden he started to talk.

'So, I bet your wondering about the whole story aren't you?' he grunted. Then carried on, 'I'm going to tell you it all. All the sordid details and then you two can choose where we go from there.' He paused for either effect or just to gloat, Sandy wasn't sure.

'Yes, you are going to have two choices. Help me escape or die! It's your choice really,' he announced, 'But first I am going to let you know what that bitch did to me. Are you comfortable?' he asked sarcastically.

Sandy wanted to be facetious back and say something like 'What do you bloody think, being tied and gagged, no we are not bloody comfortable' but of course she couldn't. You could see it in her eyes though. As they say, if looks could kill she would be a murderer right now.

Whilst Sandy was getting angry, Wanda and Tom walked into the house. Tom asked Brian to wait at the door and be their look out. Tom went in first with Wanda close behind. They walked carefully into the first room on the right. It was a lounge, very tidy and organised. There was a small table in the middle of the room with two couches and shelf unit and very little else. They left that room and went into the next one on the left. Wanda gasped as she saw a wall full of newspaper clippings, photos, diagrams and so much more. It was part shrine, part planning and part just plain evil.

'Well! We are definitely in the right house,' Tom said and then added, 'Do you want to go and get Brian, I'm sure he would like to see this. I'm going to call The Chief of Police. Be careful don't touch anything!' he ordered.

Wanda went to see Brian who was standing at the front door looking either way.

'Brian,' Wanda said, 'You wont believe what we found! You have got to come inside. I have to show you.'

Brian followed her into the strange room. They both stood at the door as Tom was on the phone. They walked in and looked around aghast. One wall was completely full of photos of Helga packed with pictures of her at school right through to a few days before she died. Another wall was full of paper cuttings and press all about her too. The really scary wall was the third. This one had loads of pictures of Sandy and Andy from the start of their investigating. Wanda suddenly saw a picture of the reporter that came to her trailer to interview her. She walked to the wall and touched a picture.

'No!' she said out loud.

'What?' said Brian.

'It doesn't matter,' said Wanda shaking her head.

Tom called Lucas and Lucas to ask where he was and explained where they were and gave him the address. He told him what they had found inside. It was then Lucas' turn and he explained that they had just received some forensic evidence from the Coroner in Curacao, where the evidence for the murder was flown to and dealt with. It seems that Helga was killed from a Taser Gun. It was hard to detect as it looked at first like a heart attack.

'Look,' Lucas said, 'We will be there in ten minutes. Make sure nothing is disturbed and if you could then go and have a look around Sandy's house to see if you can find anything that would lead us to where they are.'

Tom agreed and went into Wanda and Brian and told them that the police where coming and that he were going to go to Sandy's house next.

'I hope your taking us with you?' Wanda pleaded.

'I wasn't,' he replied, 'But I would rather take you than leave you to your own devices. I could do with an extra pair of hands anyway. For now, I think there are lots of clues on this wall to what this guy has been up to, but most important what he is going to do next?'

Wanda came up with a good idea of taking plenty of pictures, so when they leave they could refer to them. She took out her phone and clicked away, making sure she would be able to see every inch of every wall later.

Brian just stared at the pictures and said, 'This is scary! This man means business. He must be obsessed to collect all these pictures. He is deranged and that means he is dangerous. I hope they find him soon as this doesn't look good.'

All three of them turned to the forth wall. This one had pictures of the Australian zoo keeper Steve

Urwin, loads of them all about him and the way he died.

'Look!' Wanda said and added, 'Why would he put pictures up here if it didn't mean anything. I think these walls tell the story. There are childhood pictures of Helga, he must have known her for a long time.'

'Why Steve Urwin?' Brian asked as he turned the other way.

Wanda replied, 'I wonder if it's something about the way he died?'

'The Sting!' Tom shouted suddenly.

Chapter 15

Back at the cave, Phillip Jordan sat on the old broken stall and in his gruff voice, facing Sandy and Andy and started to tell his story.

'I've known that bitch since we were twelve years old. She wasn't the prim and proper tart she turned into, she was goggle eyed and red...a red head.' He seemed to think for a moment before he carried on, 'I remember our first day at school, she sat next to me and that was the first time she ignored me, bloody didn't even say hello. That's how it started and the bloody cow carried on ignoring me until she couldn't any longer. She died looking straight at me. The bitch died looking into my eyes, she'll never forget me now!'

Sandy and Andy's eyes grew larger in amazement as he told the story. They both realised he was completely crazy and Sandy's brain was working overtime on a solution to their terrible situation. She made a groan and their captor turned to her and asked, 'Shall I take the tape off?' In a peculiar and smarmy way. Sandy nodded quickly and he came over and snagged it off with no gentleness at all. Sandy stifled a scream and held her mouth to help with the pain.

'Did that hurt?' he asked sarcastically, 'Shame. Now, you can ask me any sensible questions, but be careful,' he laughed knowing he was in control. 'If you're ready, I will continue. So, she ignored me for the first time on the first day of school. I was hurt and she was the cause of that pain. I tried again when we were fifteen and got up the courage to ask her to the school dance. Do you know what that bitch fucking said? 'Who are you?' That's all she fucking said. 'Who are you?' Fucking Bitch.'

Sandy went to say something and thought better of it. Phillip didn't event notice and carried on his story. He was so engrossed he wasn't aware of much around him, until he focused on her and said.

'Wanna say something, got loads of questions? Like all bloody females, too much to bloody say. Not yet darling, you'll have your turn!' and he carried on, 'I didn't care after that rejection, didn't care about much at all. She was the cause of that.

I blame her for the next twenty-five years, when I spent most of it in bloody jail. Then the next bloody woman got her hold on me and I killed her off too!'

Sandy took an intake of breath and he heard it.

'Do you fancy being the lucky third?' he started to laugh, an ugly evil laugh.

The three friends now arrived at Sandy's house and Tom used his special tool again to open the door. They got in and split up and went into each room.

Tom went straight into the 'Murder Room' and called out to the others, 'Guys! Come in here.' Brain and Wanda walked in and saw Tom standing there with a large notepad in his hands.

'It looks like Andy has written everything down they have been up to, I have a complete log. Everything, every move they have made. This is going to be some interesting reading.'

'I hope it helps us find out where they could be.' Wanda added.

'How did you kill her?' Sandy took a chance and asked as they all sat deep in the cave.

'Which one?' he answered and laughed again, 'Helga?' He offered and Sandy nodded. 'You probably won't believe this, but it was by bloody mistake. I wanted to stun her and get my own back, make sure she noticed me and bring her here, but she bloody went and bloody died on me! Inconsiderate bitch.'

'And the other woman?' Sandy tentatively asked.

'Karen, her name was, led me on she did. She had money, loads of it, paid for a holiday, just the two of us in Antigua. She got bloody jealous when I talked to a waitress, bloody silly woman. Was about to leave her there when she begged me to stay. No one begs me! So I pushed her and she fell down the marble stairs, broke her back. I got on a boat and that's how I ended up here. Then two weeks ago I saw Helga at that restaurant I was working at. I saw her come in with a bunch of 'Lovies', he was one of them,' he said and pointed at Andy.

Andy started to make a noise as he remembered that precise moment when the waiter, now he realised it was this vile man, came over to the table and recognised Helga. Shit! He thought, if only he had known at the time, but then realised there really wasn't much he could have done. This was a mad man.

Philip looked over and huffed at Andy and carried on, 'I managed to take over as their waiter and I wanted to see what would happen when I saw her again, bloody bitch.'

Sandy wondered if he just had a very small vocabulary as his favourite words were fuck, bloody and bitch. He made a rather colourful sentence using those three words frequently.

'But this time for the last bloody time, she bloody ignored me again.' Philip slurred. 'And no one ignores me ever!'

Both sandy and Andy looked at him in part terror and part disbelief.

Tom, Brian and Wanda had now read through the first part of the log of events written by Andy.

'What are we going to do?' Wanda asked.

'We need to follow their tracks,' said Tom.

'What, to the Photographers?' asked Brian.

Before he could answer Wanda butted in with, 'Look, before we go through all that, we need to remember that whatever his name is, John, wherever he has taken them both the answer is somewhere in between this log and that horrible room. Going over all the old ground is not going to be the fastest way. We need to work out why he killed Helga and where he would of taken them and fast.'

'True,' said Tom, 'We know he knew Helga as a child, then it looks like they must have met up when she got to the island somehow, but why he killed her, I don't know.'

Wanda suggested printing out the pictures she took and putting them on the board, so that is what they proceeded to do.

At the precise moment Phillip Jorden told Sandy and Andy what he wanted them to do, 'So! You now have two choices. Death or you are going to help me get off this godforsaken island. If I was you I would choose the second choice,' and he sniggered and got up off the stall. He walked over to Andy and ripped off the tape across his mouth with sadistic pleasure.

'Ow!' Andy screamed.

'Make sure you only speak when you are spoken to,' he ordered and sort of flicked him across the head.

Andy flinched and pulled back. He wasn't good at keeping quiet and struggled to shut up. Sandy spoke up instead, as she looked at Andy with a pleading look as if to say, leave it to me, 'What are you asking us to do?' she asked softly.

'I want you to disguise me,' he said as a matter of fact as if it was easy, 'Like you did with him.' He nodded at Andy. 'That day in your trailer, I watched him go in as he is now and come out as someone else. That will do nicely. It means I can go without getting noticed and get off here, probably by boat, the way I arrived. They will all take a passenger for a bit of money. Greedy these Caribbean locals are. They will do anything for money, that's how I got the Taser. It wasn't hard, just bloody expensive.'

'How am I going to do that? I haven't got anything here?' Sandy pointed out.

'Don't be silly. We are in a bloody cave. No, I am taking the pair of you onto that film set. It's Saturday, so it will be closed, but not closed to me. We will get in, there's no health and safety here or any security except one old guy at the entrance and your going to sort him out,' he said pointing to Andy.

'Am I?' Andy answered a little bewildered.

'Now! I'm leaving you here for five minutes, just so I can get myself a car. I can't chance going out in that Toyota, they are probably scouring the whole island looking for it. I'll get myself something don't you worry. Don't get into any trouble while I'm gone,' he said and laughed that horrible evil laugh.

Both Sandy and Andy waited until he had disappeared out of the cave.

'What the fuck!' Andy said, 'How the hell are we going to get ourselves out of this, he wants to bloody kill us!'

'Andy!' Sandy whispered, 'You are starting to sound like him. Too many fucks and bloodies. Now, we have very little time to come up with a plan. Any ideas?' Sandy asked.

'Me? Ideas? Not one, except trying our hardest to stay alive. What do you suggest? Any bright ideas?' Andy quipped.

'It's no good being facetious at a time like this we need a plan and I think the best thing we can do is take our time, the longer we slow him down the longer the others can take finding us,' Sandy explained.

'How can I help with that?' Andy asked.

'I'm not sure, but I hope we find a way. I'm looking forward to working on the film,' Sandy said.

'And I'm looking forward to the rest of my life!' Andy announced, 'I'd rather it wasn't cut short.'

Chapter 16

First Tom, Brian and Wanda decided to print off the pictures and see if they could make any sense of them. They printed off twenty-two in total and pinned them up on the board. Each of them studied the pictures and came to their own conclusion. Wanda thought Phillip may have been Helga's first boyfriend and he was angry when she dumped him for another boy and he has been following her career waiting to get his own back. Brian thought Phillip might be a stalker and a mad man. It was well know Brian was a man of few words! Tom thought Phillip might be a crazed fan who lived in the same town but was never noticed by Helga. He followed her out here when he knew she was filming, but he admitted he could not understand why he would want to kill.

'Ok,' Tom said, 'Between us we have probably found out nothing, this is all assumption. We need to read these notes of Andy's and hope to God they can tell us something, so we can find them before it's too late.'

Sandy and Andy had decided the best plan was to keep their capturer as near to them as possible for as long as possible and, as long as it didn't put them in any more danger than they were in already, it would give the other guys and the police time to track them down. Well, that was the plan.

Phillip Jorden didn't take too long to get another car. He came back to the cave and told Sandy and Andy to get up and that he was going to untie the ropes, so if anyone saw them they wouldn't be suspicious, but to remember he had a gun and he wouldn't think twice before he used it. He untied the pair of them and they followed him to a car parked very close to his well-covered Toyota. They got in and Phillip started the engine after fiddling about under the dashboard.

He went slowly back over the rough terrain and onto the road. He turned right and made they made their way back over through Simpson Bay, over the hill and drove down the hill to the film set. Philip stopped half way down the hill and told

Sandy precisely what he wanted them to do when they got to the car park at the bottom. They both nodded in unison and agreed to do as they were told. They continued down the hill and parked in the car park. They all got out and walked together to the set. The same guard was on duty that Sandra had met before. They walked over to him.

'Good afternoon,' said Sandy, 'Shame we have to work on a weekend!' The guard nodded in acknowledgment and they simply walked through. They carried on until they got to Helga's old trailer where all of Sandra's makeup was stored. Philip looked around, opened the door and shoved the pair of them in roughly.

The others in Sandy's Condo had read all of Andy's notes and Brian and Wanda were not sure what to think. Both of them featured so much in the story that they were a bit bemused. It was amusing how Andy had explained his disguise and acting session as a reporter, plus their adventure with the so-called pirates. Brian wasn't at all happy that Chris, Wanda's PA, had been the instigator in that and he viewed to deal with it later.

'Look at these pictures over here,' Tom said suddenly. He pointed to a group of pictures they had printed out and put on the wall. There was a boat or yacht called 'Voyager' and a picture of Antigua and St Maarten, 'I bet he travelled here by this boat.'

I wonder if the boat is still here?' Wanda mused.

'At last there's something we can do. We can go and talk to them and find out if they know anything that can help us. I feel useless not being proactive,' Brian admitted.

'We need to find out if the boat is still in St Maarten.' Confirmed Tom, 'I just need to make a phone call before we go charging about, let me check.' Tom made a call and found out that 'Voyager' was still in St Maarten at the Marina in Simpson Bay. He picked up Andy's notebook and Wanda took the relevant pictures off the wall and all three of them left the Condo.

They drove over to Simpson bay, parked the car in the Simpson Bay Yacht Club car park and got out and walked along the footpath until they arrived at the boat. It wasn't a large boat and in amongst some of the mega yachts it looked extremely dated. St

Maarten is famous for its Mega yachts, lots of famous people moor their boats in this marina. Judge Judy, Steven Speilberg, Oprah Winfrey, to name just a few. Roman Abramovic, the owner of Chelsea Football club is the proud of owner of a few boats including the 533 foot 'Eclipse' that cost him £300million. This boat is so big it can't get into the marina and has to moor up in the bay. The Heineken regatta is held in St Maarten in March and the island plays host to hundreds of yachting enthusiasts. The three of them just stood there looking at the boat, not sure what to do next until a man walked out on the deck.

'Can I 'elp ya?' the man asked in a sort of cosmopolitan accent, maybe that of a man who has travelled around the world for many years picking up accents as he goes. He was dressed in frayed denim shorts and nothing else. Tanned and about his mid-fifties. Tom walked over and said, 'We are looking for some information about...' Tom was interrupted by his phone, as he received a text message. 'I'm sorry,' he said and checked his phone. It was a text from Lucas and a picture of the man they were all after, Phillip Jorden. Tom opened the picture and showed it to the guy on the boat, 'Have you seen this man?' he asked.

'Why? Who's asking?' the man replied.

'This man is a murderer and he has just kidnapped our two friends. If we don't find him fast they are likely to be his next victims,' Tom said in a matter of fact manner.

'Blimey!' the man replied, 'I knew there was somefin funny about 'im, but a bloody murder? Well, who'd believe it?' he said surprised.

'So you know him?' Wanda asked impatiently.

'Yeah I know 'im. Picked 'im up in Antigua. Paid me a load of cash to bring 'im 'ere. I didn't ask any questions, just let 'im come. We were coming 'ere anyway, so what did it matter earnin' a bit of cash? Kept 'imself to 'imself. Didn't ask 'im much and 'e didn't say nuffin. Sort of non-descript, sorry. Did chat to Angus though, I can get 'im and see if 'e knows anyfin. By the way, me names Todd. Todd Read. Please to met ya!' and he turned round and walked back into the boat. They all stood there silent waiting for Angus to emerge.

In the trailer Sandy had started on Philip's makeup. He insisted that she make him look twenty-five years older than he was. He told them that if she does a good enough job, he might consider letting them go. If she didn't the alternative was death. This in itself was an incentive to get it right. As she started, Sandy explained, 'This procedure normally takes up to three hours.'

'You've got forty minutes maximum and you better get it done good,' he said and then went quiet. Sandy had no choice but to do what he said. She worked harder than she had ever done before and Andy just sat there and watched with his eyes pleading that everything would be ok.

Sandy had worked wonders within the forty minutes and she transformed this man in his mid fifties to an old man of about seventy-five. No one would have recognised him from the man that came in with them. As she finished she turned him round to let him look in the mirror.

'You've done a good job,' he announced and then added, 'Now, I'm going to tie you both up again and leave you here. Someone will find you tomorrow if you are lucky,' and laughed that bloody horrible evil laugh, 'At least I'm leaving you alive.'

Both Sandy and Andy stayed quiet and hoped that he would do as he said and leave them alive.

He tied them up again, but this time back to back as they sat on the floor. He taped their mouths and said, 'Adieu and thank you for helping me get away with murder!' and left the trailer slamming the door.

It didn't take long for Angus to come out of the boat. He was a bit younger than Todd and dressed in similar old denim shorts.

'Can I help you?' he asked in a rather well spoken manner.

'We are looking for any information on this man,' Tom said as he showed him the picture on his phone.

'Ah!' said Angus, 'I'm not surprised someone is looking for him. He reminded me of a sewer rat, evil looking and smarmy. I'm not sure I can tell you much, he didn't really say a lot. I know he has spent most of his life in and out of prison. He doesn't have any family and he's conniving. That's it really, that's all the personal stuff he told me. He will find a way to get what he wants and go to any lengths to get it. It's in his makeup.'

They were all silent for a moment.

'Makeup?' Wanda repeated. 'That's it! That's what Andy did, didn't he? Sandy made him up so that he could interview me and this John knows it too, he took pictures. I bet he is going to get Sandy to do the same to him as she did for Andy, so that he can escape. He wants to use a makeup artiste to create a disguise for him!'

Angus looked bemused at Wanda's tirade and said, 'Ok Guys, that all I can help with,' and made his way back onto the boat.

Brian turned to Tom and said, 'Looks like she may have a point. So, where would they do that?' he turned to ask Wanda, as if she knew everything.

'I'm guessing all Sandy's stuff is at the set. Probably still in Helga's old trailer waiting for the new actor to turn up,' Wanda suggested.

'Ok, it looks like we are off to catch a killer. Thanks for your help!' Tom shouted as Angus was making his way back on to the boat. All three of them turned and ran back to the car. Just before they got in Tom said, 'I've got to call Lucas and tell him our suspicions.'

'Shame, I would have liked to finish this off with us saving Sandy and Andy,' Wanda lamented.

Tom called Lucas and explained what they had been up to and Wanda's suspicions about Philip using Sandy as a makeup artiste. Also, that they think they may all be all on the film set. Lucas straight away shouted to someone else in his office and gave instructions for the police to go immediately to the film set.

'Ok, Tom,' he said, 'Leave this one to us. As I said before he may be armed.' Tom agreed but Brian and Wanda saw him cross his fingers. He put the phone down to Lucas and announced, 'There is no way we are just sitting here and letting the police finish the job without seeing the outcome and helping Sandy and Andy. Come on guys, get in.' They all jumped in the car and drove off towards the film set.

It was all quiet after Philip left. Sandy couldn't quite believe that he had just left them, but also realised that for him it was just self-survival and his only probable chance of escape. Andy looked tired and drained. He was just sitting there nodding his head. Sandy tried loosening the tape across her mouth. She used her tongue to moisten the stickiness and managed to loosen the side. She must have looked ridiculous and the funny noises she was making changed Andy's mood. He started to laugh, albeit not being able to move his mouth. Sandy realised how silly she must have looked and sounded, but carried on with the procedure. Suddenly she was free, well her mouth was and the tape hung half on and half off.

'Thank Fuck!' she spurted out.

Andy tried laughing even harder and this had the desired effect. His tape also snapped of on one side.

'I concur!' he shouted, 'Thank Fuck!' and they both laughed out loud. At the same time they heard a gunshot and the laughter stopped.

Tom, Wanda and Brian were driving down the steep slope to the film set and pulled up sharply as they could see the police standing by their cars with guns facing their target, an old man carrying a gun. They watched the story unfold in front of them as they couldn't hear what was happening, they were too far away and safely inside the car. Wanda went to get out the car and Brian stopped her by flying across her lap and preventing her from opening the door.

'I don't think so young lady! You can stay in here and no arguing. This isn't the time to get involved, this is now for the police to deal with.'

Wanda desperately wanted to get out and see if she could find Sandy and Andy, but she wasn't silly and realised she would have to wait. She felt that someone needed to find them and see what had happened to them, the not knowing was awful. Also knowing that the man down the hill, who now looked like an old man, was capable of murder. He had already murdered one person, but had he murdered two more? Were her friends alive or dead, she desperately wanted to know.

Two officers were poised with guns pointing at Philip Jorden. He may have looked like an old man, but his voice couldn't be disguised. He had his gun pointed at the police car and was shouting at them.

'I'm not giving up, so you'll have to shoot me. I don't bloody care anymore. Go on! You haven't got the bloody guts have you, well take this!' Philip Jorden lifted his gun, but the police officers were too fast and shot him first. Only one shot, in the leg, Philip fell and screamed in pain and the gun fell too. The other officer ran over to retrieve the gun. It was over.

Wanda had been holding her breath, she saw the man fall and let out a sigh and opened the car door and started running. She went past all the commotion and was followed close behind by Brian, who was also running to keep up with her. They passed the tents and Wanda's trailer until they got to Helga's old trailer. Wanda put her hand on the handle but didn't turn it.

'I'm not religious, but I hope to God they are ok Brian,' she whispered.

'Hello!' They heard a voice shout, before Wanda had a chance to open the door.

'I think God heard you,' Brian answered and Wanda opened the door to see Sandy and Andy sitting on the floor tied up.

'About bloody time too!' Andy said as he let out a whimper.

'Well, that's gratitude for you,' said Wanda going in and trying to take off Andy's rope and the remainder of the tape. Brain was dealing with Sandy as they both tried talking at the same time.

'Woah! One at a time,' Wanda said loudly, so they both listened. Sandy stood up and stretched her muscles.

'Thank you! You are a site for sore eyes, we thought we were on our way out!'

'Being bloody detectives,' Andy said loudly, 'I'm giving that one up! I thought it was fun at first but he was bloody evil. Bloody hell! Whatever happens Sandy I'm not getting into any more bloody adventures with you, I have had enough 'adventures' to last a bloody life time!'

'Can you get anymore 'bloody's in to one sentence?' Sandy asked.

'I probably bloody can,' he answered and they all laughed and left the trailer.

Chapter 17

They were all standing outside talking at the same time until Tom spoke up and said, 'Will the lot of you shut up!' It went silent and they all laughed.

'Now, I'm sure you would just like to get home have a shower and forget everything, but I'm afraid you are going to have to recall everything as the police want to speak to you.'

'Shit,' Andy said loudly.

'Andy!' Sandy said and gave him a friendly slap on the arm and they all laughed again.

'At least you are safe,' Wanda said, 'We were so worried about you both.'

'Not as much as we were with a bloody gun pointed at us. I was bloody terrified,' Andy told them.

'Some of that mad gunman's language has rubbed off on you Andy,' Sandy admonished him.

'How did you know where to find us?' Sandy asked them.

'I guessed!' said Wanda feeling rather clever.

'How?' Sandy and Andy said at the same time.

'We have read your log Andy. Very interesting reading especially the part about that lovely reporter that came to interview me,' Wanda confessed.

'Whoops!' said Andy and then added, 'I'm sorry,' and continued with, 'All part of the world of investigation I'm afraid.' Wanda laughed it off.

'Plus the 'Pirate' abduction. That was my favourite part,' Brian added.

Wanda's phone made a noise as she received a text. She read it and laughed again. 'You are not going to believe this timing,' Wanda announced, as the rest waited in anticipation.

'Well?' said Andy.

'That was Stuart my makeup artiste. His mother has been taken ill and he is going home.'

It went silent and all eyes went first to Sandy and then to Wanda.

'Now Sandy, I've seen what you can do with makeup. Creating Andy as the reporter and that madman as a geriatric, so in a way you've had a trial! Would you consider working for me? It would mean working full time and travelling around the world, what do you think?'

Sandy took a nano second to nod like one of those dogs in the back of a car. Everyone looked happy, except Andy.

Brian turned to him and said, 'After that Pirate business Chris will not be working as Wanda's PA anymore. I am not happy and neither will the Director be when he finds out that Chris used the film's boat to play a silly prank. So Andy...' Brian didn't get a chance to finish what he was trying to say.

'I would love to be your PA Wanda!' Andy gushed, ignoring Brian.

'Well it's lucky that that was what I was going to ask you then,' said Brian smiling.

'So now you are all the best of friends and are all safe, can I take you to Lucas and his team so they can talk to you?' Tom asked and they all followed as he led the way out.

They spent about three hours with the police and then they were dismissed. Tom took them all back to their relevant homes and they arranged to go out for dinner at Bamboo Bernies, as they had missed out on lunch.

Sandy walked into her lovely Caribbean home and sat on the porch and sighed. She thought about everything that had happened in just one short week and mentally put it in a box of experience. Closed that chapter and wondered what the new one would bring. It was time for Sandy to bring an end to this crazy mad week and she now knew she had a bright, if maybe hectic and crazy, life ahead. Who knows what was to happen in the future. But one thing she did know was, was sure looking forward to it!